WITHDRAWN

It's her!

"There's Ashley!" Mr. Sutton said excitedly.

As she looked where her father was pointing, Amy drew in a sharp breath. *She's gorgeous,* Amy thought.

Ashley was tall and slender, with reddish-brown hair, big blue eyes, and a perfect complexion. *She looks like Dad,* Amy realized in amazement.

Ashley approached them with an enormous smile and outstretched arms. "Dad!" she cried, flinging her arms around Mr. Sutton. "I could tell it was you right away from the pictures Mom showed me."

Amy stood frozen as her father and this beautiful girl shared a warm embrace. *Dad,* she repeated to herself. She had a funny feeling in her stomach hearing her father called that by somebody else. But what difference does it make what Ashley calls him? *Amy thought. He is her dad, too.*

Ashley drew back from Mr. Sutton's arms to gaze at her. "And you must be my sister, Amy!"

Amy thought she would burst with emotion as she and her sister hugged each other and their father enveloped the two of them in his arms.

SWEET VALLEY TWINS are published by Bantam Books.
Ask your bookseller for titles you have missed:

SWEET VALLEY TWINS

Amy's Secret Sister

Written by
Jamie Suzanne

Created by
FRANCINE PASCAL

BANTAM BOOKS
TORONTO · NEW YORK · LONDON · SYDNEY · AUCKLAND

AMY'S SECRET SISTER
A BANTAM BOOK   0 553 40828 **3**

Originally published in USA by Bantam Books

First publication in Great Britain

PRINTING HISTORY
Bantam edition published 1995

The trademarks "Sweet Valley" and "Sweet Valley Twins"
are owned by Francine Pascal and are used under license by
Bantam Books and Transworld Publishers Ltd.

Conceived by Francine Pascal.

Produced by Daniel Weiss Associates, Inc,
33 West 17th Street, New York, NY 10011

All rights reserved.

Copyright © 1994 by Francine Pascal
Cover art copyright © 1994 by Daniel Weiss Associates, Inc.

Cover art by James Mathewuse

Conditions of sale
1. This book is sold subject to the condition that it shall not,
by way of trade or otherwise, be lent, re-sold, hired out
or otherwise circulated without the publisher's prior consent
in any form of binding or cover other than that in which it is
published and without a similar condition including this
condition being imposed on the subsequent purchaser.
2. This book is sold subject to the Standard Conditions of Sale
of Net Books and may not be re-sold in the UK below the net price
fixed by the publishers for the book.

Bantam Books are published by Transworld Publishers Ltd,
61–63 Uxbridge Road, Ealing, London W5 5SA,
in Australia by Transworld Publishers (Australia) Pty Ltd,
15–25 Helles Avenue, Moorebank, NSW 2170,
and in New Zealand by Transworld Publishers (NZ) Ltd,
3 William Pickering Drive, Albany, Auckland.

Printed and bound in Great Britain by
Cox & Wyman Ltd, Reading, Berkshire

To Nicole Pascal Johansson

514099

MORAY DISTRICT COUNCIL
DEPARTMENT OF
LEISURE AND LIBRARIES
JC

One

"Amy, honey, your mom and I need to have a private talk with you," Mr. Sutton said in a somber tone. "I'm sorry, Elizabeth. Do you mind heading home a little early tonight?"

Amy Sutton felt her heart constrict. It was Tuesday night, and she was having dinner at her house with her parents and her best friend, Elizabeth Wakefield. For the past couple of weeks, Amy had been afraid something was wrong with her parents. She had even confessed to Elizabeth that she thought her parents were heading for a divorce.

And when she and Elizabeth did some investigating in Mr. Sutton's office, her worst fears were confirmed. The girls discovered an unsent letter addressed to someone named Jane and pictures of Mr.

Sutton with his arm around another woman.

And disaster had struck in the middle of dinner that night, when Amy had answered the phone. It was a woman named Jane, calling for Mr. Sutton. He had talked to her for a few minutes and come back into the dining room with a gloomy expression on his face.

"N-no. Not at all," Elizabeth responded, getting up from the table. "I . . . uh . . . have a lot of home-work tonight, anyway," she mumbled.

Amy numbly walked Elizabeth to the front door and said good-bye. When she returned to the dining room, her father had taken his seat at the table. Amy's parents gazed at her as she sat down. Amy felt as though the room were closing in around her. *I can't believe it's really happening*, she thought as she sat motionless in her chair. *They're going to tell me our family is breaking up.*

"Amy, we have something very important we need to discuss with you," Mr. Sutton said care-fully.

"C-can't we talk about it tomorrow?" Amy asked in a choked voice. "I have a lot of homework, too."

"We need to talk about it now," Mr. Sutton said.

Amy looked at her mother and then at her father. She had never seen them look so serious before. She felt a lump rising in her throat and fought back the tears that were welling in her eyes.

"You're getting a divorce!" Amy blurted out.

"What? What are you talking about?" Mrs. Sutton asked, looking at Mr. Sutton with a confused expression.

"Isn't that what you wanted to tell me?" Amy asked in a wobbling voice. "Isn't that why you've been acting so strange lately?"

"Oh, honey," Mr. Sutton said, reaching across the table and taking Amy's hand. "Your mother and I are as much in love today as we were the day we got married. Nothing's going to change that."

Amy let out a long breath, trying to release all the tension and anxiety of the last few days. "But what could be so terrible, then?" she asked, almost afraid to feel relieved yet.

"Amy, I'm sorry we've given you the impression it's something terrible," Mr. Sutton said slowly. "It's actually wonderful news. It just might take you a little while to get used to it, that's all."

Her parents' eyes met for a moment. Mr. Sutton cleared his throat. Mrs. Sutton drew in a deep breath.

"Amy . . ." Mrs. Sutton began.

"This is going to come as quite a surprise," Mr. Sutton broke in.

"You see . . ." Mrs. Sutton said, crumpling up her napkin in her fist.

". . . you have a sister," Mr. Sutton finished.

"I feel awful for Amy," Elizabeth said to her twin sister, Jessica, collapsing on Jessica's bed.

Elizabeth had left the Suttons' house just an hour before and had knocked on Jessica's door when she couldn't even pretend to concentrate on her math homework any longer. She couldn't get the image of Amy's scared, sad face out of her head.

Jessica looked back at her from where she stood at the mirror. "What do you think of my hair like this?" Jessica asked. She had pulled the two front sections of her long, shiny blond hair back with barrettes. "I'm trying out different hairstyles from that book of international hair that I bought. This is called a Greek Surprise."

Elizabeth sighed. "Didn't you hear what I was saying? I'm afraid Amy's finding out right now that her parents are getting divorced."

Even though Jessica and Elizabeth were identical twins, their similarities were only on the outside. They both had long, silky blond hair, blue-green eyes, and a dimple in their left cheek. They were both beautiful girls, but Jessica was much more preoccupied with her looks than Elizabeth. In fact, sometimes Jessica's concern about her appearance got on Elizabeth's nerves.

Elizabeth was more serious than Jessica about most things, including schoolwork. She worked on one of the two school newspapers, *The Sweet Valley Sixers*, and hoped to be a writer when she grew up. She loved reading mysteries and having long talks with her friends.

Jessica, on the other hand, was a member of the

Unicorn Club, a group of the prettiest and most popular girls in Sweet Valley Middle School. Elizabeth thought they were silly. It seemed that all they ever talked about was boys, parties, clothes, and the latest gossip.

"Yeah, I heard you," Jessica said in a bored tone as she took out her barrettes and flipped her hair upside down. "I just don't see what the point is of sitting around worrying whether Amy Sutton's parents are getting a divorce. It's not like there's anything you can do about it."

"That's not a very nice attitude, Jessica," Elizabeth said. "You *could* be a little more understanding."

"How do you like it like this?" Jessica was holding her hair on top of her head in a loose bun. "Don't you think it makes me look older?"

"Yes, you look like you're sixty-five," Elizabeth replied. "Now you'll get the senior-citizen discount at the movies."

"Har-dee-har-har," Jessica said, rolling her eyes.

"Elizabeth!" Mrs. Wakefield yelled from downstairs. "Amy's here to see you!"

Elizabeth felt her stomach do a backflip. "Oh, my gosh! What should I say to Amy?" she whispered

"Don't ask me," Jessica said, still brushing her hair in front of the mirror. "Like I said, if they're getting a divorce, nothing you say to Amy will make any difference. It's a done deal."

"Boy, that's really comforting," Elizabeth said on

her way out the door. "And by the way, you look ridiculous with your hair like that."

Elizabeth closed the door behind her and walked slowly down the stairs, dreading the conversation she was about to have.

"Hi, Amy," Elizabeth said, hesitating at the door of the Wakefields' family room.

Amy was standing with her back to Elizabeth, staring out the window. Elizabeth felt a flood of sympathy for her friend as she looked at her limp, blond hair falling just above her shoulders. Elizabeth couldn't help thinking about Jessica, who was upstairs playing with her hair at that very moment. Compared with what Amy was going through, Jessica's obsession with her hair seemed especially trivial.

Elizabeth braced herself as Amy turned around, sure that Amy's face would be covered with tears. But to Elizabeth's shock, Amy was smiling radiantly.

"Elizabeth!" Amy ran over to her friend and gave her a big hug. "I have the best news!"

Elizabeth gasped. How could there possibly be great news, when just a few hours before, the tension at Amy's house had been practically unbearable? *Maybe she's so upset that she's gone into some hysterical kind of state*, Elizabeth thought with concern. "Amy, sit down." Elizabeth led her over to the couch and sat her down. "Now, take your time and tell me what's going on. Are you feeling OK? Do you want some soda or something?"

"I've never felt better," Amy said.

"OK," Elizabeth said in a calm, levelheaded voice, as she took Amy's hands. "Why don't you take a deep breath and start at the beginning."

"Well, you know the woman we saw in those pictures and the one he addressed that letter to?"

"Of course," Elizabeth said. "Jane."

"Right," Amy went on. "And she was also the one who called tonight."

Elizabeth nodded and looked at Amy expectantly.

"Well," Amy continued brightly, "she and my dad were high school sweethearts, and they got married when they were very young. My dad said they were too young, and the marriage just didn't work out."

"Oh, my gosh!" Elizabeth exclaimed. She was completely stunned. But even more incredible than the news itself was how ecstatic Amy looked about it. *If I found out that one of my parents had been married before, I think I'd feel really strange,* she thought. "When did the marriage break up?" she managed to choke out.

"Well, a few years after they'd gotten married, my dad was offered a job as a photographer in Singapore," Amy said eagerly. "He took the assignment, and Jane decided to stay in America with her family."

"Amy, I don't even know what to say. This

whole thing is just so incredible," Elizabeth said, her eyes widening.

"You haven't even heard the *really* incredible part!" Amy said excitedly.

"What could be more incredible than finding out that your father was married to someone else before your mother?" Elizabeth asked in disbelief.

"Just wait till you hear the rest," Amy said. "So my father stayed in Singapore, and he and Jane got divorced and lost touch. He met my mother, who was working there as a broadcast journalist. They fell in love and got married."

"And had you," Elizabeth added.

"Exactly," Amy said, beaming. "Anyway, when I was five years old, my father found out from Jane that he had another daughter, who was a year and a half older than me."

Elizabeth's mouth fell open in amazement. "You're kidding!" she exclaimed. "And your mother just found out about it now? No wonder she's seemed so upset lately!"

"No, that's not it," Amy said brightly. "My mother has known about it all along, but my parents wanted to wait until I was older to tell me. The main reason they've been so gloomy lately is that they've been worried about how I might take the news. Isn't that sweet?"

"Well, it *is* big news," Elizabeth said carefully. "I can see why they'd be afraid you'd have trouble adjusting—"

Amy didn't seem to be listening. "My sister's name is Ashley, and the best part of all is that she's coming here on Thursday evening! She's going to stay with us for two whole weeks!"

"This Thursday?" Elizabeth asked. *Amy certainly has a lot to deal with all at once*, she thought. "That's so soon."

"My parents wanted her to come even sooner, but it took them a while to convince Jane to let Ashley come—that's the other reason they were in such bad moods. Jane was being difficult, because she didn't want Ashley to miss school. But my parents arranged for her to take classes with me while she's here. Isn't it wonderful?"

Elizabeth felt completely overwhelmed. Discovering you had a sister *could* be wonderful, of course, but Elizabeth thought it could also be really unsettling. "It's really amazing," she told Amy. "It's like something from that soap opera Jessica's always watching."

"I've always wanted a sister," Amy continued dreamily. "Did I mention she'll be staying in my room with me? Oh, my gosh!" Amy jumped off the couch. "I should go home right now and start fixing it up."

"Um, Amy," Elizabeth called as her friend hurried to the door.

"Yeah?" Amy asked eagerly, turning around.

"I just wanted to warn you that, well, as wonderful as it is to have a sister, it can also be a pain sometimes. In fact, there are days when I wish I were an only child."

"Oh, you don't have to worry about me," Amy said reassuringly. "I've been an only child my whole life. I'm ready to find out what it's like to have a sister!"

But Elizabeth couldn't help worrying as she watched her friend skipping from her doorstep down the walkway. *I just hope she stays this happy after she finds out what it's really like to have a sister,* Elizabeth thought.

Two

"Guess what? My mom and I went to the mall yesterday and bought matching bedspreads for the twin beds in my room," Amy told Elizabeth excitedly. It was Thursday morning, and they were sitting at their desks waiting for Mrs. Arnette to start social studies class.

"I thought you already had matching bedspreads," Elizabeth said, taking her pencil and eraser out of her plastic zipper bag.

"I had those pink flowered bedspreads, but they were so babyish," Amy said. "I didn't want Ashley to think I was a total loser. My mom didn't want to buy new ones, but I begged her nonstop for two hours, and she finally gave in."

"So what do the new ones look like?"

"They're very simple but very sophisticated,"

Amy said. "They just have black and white stripes with red polka dots thrown around here and there. Ashley's in the seventh grade, and I want her to think I have mature taste."

At that moment Jessica flew into the classroom and plopped down in her usual seat next to Elizabeth.

Elizabeth glanced casually at her sister, then looked again. Jessica was wearing Elizabeth's new ruffled blue blouse. "I really can't believe you sometimes," Elizabeth whispered angrily as Mrs. Arnette started taking attendance.

"What are you talking about?" Jessica asked innocently.

"You know exactly what I'm talking about," Elizabeth said hotly. "You knew I was saving that shirt for a special occasion. I haven't even worn it yet."

"I was wearing it this morning at breakfast and you didn't say anything about it," Jessica said, twirling her hair with her finger.

"That's because you were wearing a sweater over it," Elizabeth told her. She wasn't possessive about her belongings, but she couldn't stand it when Jessica took her clothes without asking. Why did her sister always have to take her newest, nicest things?

Elizabeth leaned toward Amy. "As you can see, having a sister isn't all it's cracked up to be."

"I can't wait to argue over clothes like that with

my sister," Amy said, smiling. "It seems like the kind of thing sisters are supposed to fight about."

"See?" Jessica said to Elizabeth. "I'm just doing what a sister's supposed to do."

Elizabeth rolled her eyes. "If you really start to like this sister thing and want another one, I'll be glad to give you mine for a while."

"I can't believe none of you said anything about my new hairdo," Jessica said between bites of her hamburger. It was lunchtime on Thursday, and Jessica was sitting with her fellow Unicorns in the Unicorner, their usual table in the school cafeteria.

"Don't tell me," Lila Fowler said, pretending to study Jessica's hair closely. "You washed it."

Lila was the wealthiest girl in Sweet Valley and lived in an enormous mansion. Even though she was Jessica's best friend after Elizabeth, the two were super-competitive with each other. Everyone at the table laughed at Lila's joke except Jessica.

"Gee, Lila, did you ever consider pursuing a career as a stand-up comedian?" Jessica asked. "You're so hysterically funny. I'm sure you'd be a big hit."

Lila ignored Jessica's comment and bit into a french fry.

"So, what *is* different about your hair?" Ellen Riteman asked.

"I have this new book of hairstyles from around the world, and today I'm trying something called a

Norwegian Lift." Jessica puffed up the back of her hair with her right hand.

"But it looks the way it always does," Janet Howell said. Janet was the president of the Unicorns and an eighth-grader. All the Unicorns, especially Jessica, wanted her approval.

"What exactly are we supposed to notice about it?" Lila asked.

"If you can't tell from looking at it, then I'm not going to explain it," Jessica said, slightly hurt. She had spent a half hour in the bathroom that morning trying to perfect the style. She'd teased it on top just the way they'd said to in the book. She was beginning to wish she'd never brought up the subject of her hair in the first place.

"No offense, but don't we have anything better to discuss than Jessica's hair?" Tamara Chase asked. She covered her mouth and pretended to yawn. "Doesn't anyone have any good gossip?"

The Unicorns looked at one another blankly.

What a total bore this is, Jessica thought. Even though she loved being a Unicorn, she had to admit that eating lunch with the same people day after day sometimes got a little old. They were all so used to one another that they couldn't recognize a really cool hairstyle when they saw one. Suddenly an idea popped into Jessica's head. "I think we need some new blood."

Everyone looked at Jessica as if she'd announced she was joining the chess club.

"You mean, like, a new member?" Janet asked. "Why would we want that?"

"Yeah, really," Tamara agreed, peering at Jessica.

"I think we could liven things up a little bit if we had someone new to hang out with," Jessica said enthusiastically.

Lila scrunched up her face as if she'd just eaten something sour.

"Our club is full enough as it is," Janet announced authoritatively.

"Well, we could bring in a temporary member, kind of on a trial basis or something," Jessica suggested. "If it doesn't work out, then we'll tell them to take a hike."

"You know," Ellen said thoughtfully, "it might not be a bad idea to have a new member for a while."

"See?" Jessica said, looking eagerly around the table. "Ellen agrees with me."

"At least if we had a new member we could probably figure out something to talk about besides Jessica's hair," Ellen continued.

"Yeah, good point," Kimberly Haver said.

"It might be kind of fun to get to know someone new," Mandy Miller added.

"Hmm, new blood." Janet strummed her fingers on the table as she considered the idea. "This matter is of extreme importance," she said finally. "I say we vote. All those in favor of letting in a new temporary Unicorn raise their right hand."

Every hand went up except Lila's. "I really think you guys are making a mistake," Lila said. "As soon as we open up our door to the whole school, we risk losing our exclusivity."

"Sorry, Lila, but majority rules," Jessica said, smiling sweetly. She was thrilled that the Unicorns, and especially Janet, had sided with her against Lila.

"Does anyone have any ideas about who would be good Unicorn material?" Janet asked.

"That's a tough one," Tamara said. "Anyone who's cool enough to be a Unicorn already is one."

"We'll just all have to keep our eyes open," Jessica said. "There must be someone in this school who's qualified."

"Once word gets out that we're scouting for a new Unicorn, we'll never be left alone," Lila complained. "Every girl in school will be trying to impress us."

Yeah, and maybe we'll find someone who will be impressed by my funky hairstyles, Jessica thought as she scanned the cafeteria for possibilities.

"Did you hear the latest news?" Amy asked Elizabeth in the office of *The Sweet Valley Sixers* on Thursday afternoon.

Elizabeth looked up from the story she was editing. "Something we should put in the paper?"

"Maybe you should ask your sister about that," Amy said.

"My sister? Why would I ever ask Jessica about what to put in the *Sixers*?" Elizabeth laughed. Jessica knew as much about newspapers as Elizabeth knew about soap operas—absolutely nothing.

"It's about the Unicorns," Amy said excitedly.

"Don't tell me. One of the Unicorns broke a fingernail," Elizabeth joked.

Amy giggled. "No, they're opening up a position in their club. They're starting a search for a new Unicorn," she said.

"Oh, no, don't tell me they're expanding again," Elizabeth groaned. "Aren't there more than enough of them as it is? They're going to take over Sweet Valley."

"They're not exactly expanding. They're just looking for one more girl to be a temporary member," Amy explained.

"Who would ever want to be a Unicorn?"

"I would," Amy almost whispered.

Elizabeth put down her pencil. "Excuse me, I must be hearing things today. I thought I heard you say you wanted to be a Unicorn."

"You're not hearing things," Amy said with a laugh. "I know I've never been too interested in the Unicorns, but talking to Ashley on the phone last night made me change my mind."

"You talked to her? That's great! Why didn't you tell me?" *And what on earth could she have said that makes you want to a Unicorn?* Elizabeth wondered silently.

Amy giggled. "I guess I was saving the news. We only talked for a few minutes, but it was so great to hear my own sister's voice. She told me a little about her school and her friends. She belongs to a group at her school in New York that sounds a lot like the Unicorns."

"Well, um, that's great," Elizabeth said. "But I don't see exactly what this has to do with your wanting to be a Unicorn."

"Don't worry, I'm not talking about forever—just while my sister's here. I mean, obviously Ashley's popular, and you have to admit, my social life isn't exactly thrilling. I think Ashley would be impressed if I were a member of the most popular group in school."

"Amy, your sister will be impressed with you just the way you are," Elizabeth said, pushing a loose strand of hair back into her ponytail. "You have so much going for you. You're way too smart to be a Unicorn."

"Your own sister is a Unicorn," Amy pointed out.

"Yeah, but you're different from Jessica, and so am I," Elizabeth said. "We have more important things to think about than parties and clothes."

"Look, I know how you feel about the Unicorns, and normally I agree with you," Amy said slowly. "But it would really mean a lot to me to be one while Ashley's here." She took a deep breath. "And actually, there's something I wanted to ask you. I was wondering if you'd mind putting in a word for me with your sister."

Elizabeth bit her lip. She knew what Jessica's reaction would be if she suggested Amy as a Unicorn. Jessica thought Amy was boring and kind of klutzy. She wouldn't even consider it. "Believe me, you're much better off steering clear of that silly club." *And I hope that's the end of it, because there's not much chance you'll become one,* Elizabeth added silently.

Amy's heart was beating fast and her palms were sweaty. It was Thursday night, and Amy and Mr. Sutton had driven to the airport to pick up Ashley. *I can't believe I'm about to meet my sister,* she thought. *In just a few minutes I'll meet a girl who will be in my life forever.*

"D-do you think that's her?" Amy asked her father as she pointed to a girl with brown hair and glasses.

"That girl looks too young," Mr. Sutton said. "Remember, Ashley's a year and a half older than you are."

Amy's stomach was full of butterflies. She'd never been so nervous in her life. *What if we have nothing in common? What if Ashley doesn't like me?*

Amy anxiously looked down at her outfit. She had spent two hours getting ready, trying on dozens of different outfits before deciding on a pair of jeans and her favorite long-sleeved green T-shirt.

Amy looked up as another rush of passengers came down the corridor. "What about that girl in the straw hat?" Amy asked, pointing to a gawky girl with long blond hair. "She looks about the right age."

"No, that girl's with her parents. Ashley's traveling alone," Mr. Sutton pointed out.

The more people who piled through the gate doors, the more excited and nervous Amy got. She felt as if she were about to explode. Then her father touched her arm.

"There's Ashley," he said excitedly.

As she looked where her father was pointing, Amy drew in a big breath. *She's gorgeous*, she thought.

Ashley was tall and slender, with reddish-brown hair, big blue eyes, and a perfect complexion. *She looks like one of Mom's porcelain dolls*, Amy thought. *She also looks a little like Dad*, she realized in amazement.

Ashley approached them with an enormous smile and outstretched arms. "Dad!" she cried, flinging her arms around Mr. Sutton. "I could tell it was you right away from the pictures Mom showed me."

Amy stood frozen as her father and this beautiful girl shared a warm embrace. *Dad*, she repeated to herself. She had a funny feeling in her stomach hearing her father called that by somebody else. *She'd* been the only person ever to call him that. But her father obviously didn't mind. Amy saw that his eyes were filled with tears.

But what difference does it make what Ashley calls him? she thought. *He is her dad, too. And what's most important is that my sister is standing right here next to me.* She smiled eagerly as Ashley drew back from Mr. Sutton's arms to gaze at her. "And you must be my sister, Amy!"

Amy thought she would burst with emotion as she and her sister hugged each other and their father enveloped the two of them in his arms.

Three

"I love your room," Ashley said to Amy as she unpacked her bags. "It's so nice of you to let me share it with you."

As she watched Ashley move around her bedroom excitedly, Amy kept reminding herself that she wasn't dreaming. *This girl right here in front of me is really my half sister*, she told herself.

"I'm so happy you like it," Amy said proudly. "I wanted it to look nice for you."

Ashley sat down on the bed next to Amy and put her arm around her. "I feel like there's so much we have to catch up on. I want to know everything about you."

Amy smiled at her sister. "I'm worried there's not that much to tell. I'm basically pretty average. I like sports, I write for the school newspaper, and I guess I'm a pretty good student. Sounds boring, I guess."

"Are you kidding? It's so cool that you write for the newspaper," Ashley said.

"You really think so?"

"Definitely," Ashley said, pulling a hairbrush out of her makeup bag. She began to brush her beautiful hair. Amy looked at it longingly. She had always wanted wavy hair. Amy's hair tended to be limp, but Ashley's was shiny and wavy at the same time.

"So what do you do for fun?" Ashley asked. "Do you have a boyfriend?"

Amy blushed. "Well, I guess I have a sort-of boyfriend."

"What's his name?"

"Ken Matthews."

"What's he like?" Ashley asked.

"He's a sixth-grader, and he's pretty cute," Amy said, still gazing at Ashley's hair, which was falling in ripples around her face. "What about you? Do you have a boyfriend?"

"Actually, I have a few boyfriends," Ashley said. She jumped up and took a small photo album from one of her bags. She handed the album to Amy.

Amy turned to the first page. "Oh, my gosh, he's totally gorgeous!" she exclaimed, staring at a photograph of a blond, blue-eyed guy in a bathing suit, who looked at least fifteen.

"That's Peter," Ashley said, shaking her head.

"I don't know what to do about him."

"What do you mean?"

"He's so possessive and jealous that he drives me absolutely crazy," Ashley said. "I'm always telling him that I'm not interested in going out with only one person, but he doesn't get it."

"I can't imagine that there could be anyone cuter at your school that you'd want to go out with," Amy said.

"You haven't seen Josh yet." Ashley flipped to the next picture, of a boy with longish black hair and deep-green eyes.

"Wow! Is he your boyfriend, too?" Amy asked. "He is even cuter than Peter."

"Check out Scott." Ashley flipped to a picture of a tall, muscular guy with gorgeous dark-red hair.

"What kind of school do you go to?" Amy asked. "A school for models?"

Ashley laughed as she put the album away.

For a moment Amy thought about Ken. He was cute and everything, but compared with Ashley's boyfriends, he seemed like a little kid. *I can't imagine what that would be like, to have so many incredible-looking guys interested in me,* Amy thought.

"You know, it's funny," Ashley said, breaking into Amy's thoughts. "I've always wanted a sister."

"Really? Me, too. In fact, when I was little, I used to pretend that I *did* have a sister," Amy said, blushing.

Ashley's eyes widened. "That's so funny. So did

I! My pretend little sister was named Samantha," Ashley said. "I even used to throw birthday parties for her. And at dinnertime I made my mother put food on a plate for Samantha."

Amy laughed. "No way! I did that kind of thing all the time," Amy said with a laugh. "One time I was at a movie with my dad. I mean, um . . ." Amy paused and cleared her throat. "I mean, our dad. Anyway, the theater was totally full when we got there, so we took the last two seats on the aisle. I wouldn't sit down, because I didn't think it was fair that Susie, my pretend sister, couldn't sit, too. My dad—our dad—sat in one of the seats, and I sat in the aisle for practically the whole movie."

Both girls started to laugh hysterically.

"Our families must have thought we were totally nuts," Ashley said.

"Yeah," Amy agreed. "I never thought of it before, but I guess I was a pretty weird kid."

"I was a pretty weird kid, too," Ashley said. "Maybe that's why we're getting along so well. We're both a little weird."

Amy smiled at her sister. "Having a make-believe sister was fun, but the real thing is about a hundred times better."

"These are delicious," Ashley said, biting into a big, soft chocolate-chip cookie later that night.

"I'm glad you like them," Mrs. Sutton said.

Amy and Ashley were sitting at the kitchen

table, having hot chocolate and cookies with Mr. and Mrs. Sutton before going to bed.

"These are my absolute favorite," Amy said, helping herself to her third cookie. "Mom only makes these on special occasions, so it's a good thing you're here." She smiled. "I mean, that's not the *only* reason I'm glad you're here."

"We're *all* so happy you're here, Ashley," Mrs. Sutton said. "We want you to feel like you're part of our family."

"I already do feel like part of the family," Ashley said. "And I'm psyched to go to school with Amy."

"That reminds me," Mr. Sutton said. "At your mom's suggestion, we signed you up for classes at the Sweet Valley Dance Studio while you're here. Your mom told me on the phone that you're a wonderful ballerina."

Ashley's face lit up. "That's super," she said gratefully. "I was a little worried about getting out of shape while I'm here." She heaved a contented sigh as a warm breeze drifted through the window. "Gosh, I can't believe I'm actually in California. I've wanted to come here for the longest time. I've never even been away from the East Coast before."

"We'll have to give you the Sweet Valley tour," Mr. Sutton said. "Amy's a good tour guide."

"I don't know about that," Amy said, feeling a little timid. "I mean, there's not a whole lot to see here. Especially compared with New York City."

"Believe me, just seeing tall trees in your front

yard is pretty thrilling," Ashley said. "The trees on the streets of New York are almost all little stunted things."

"I love New York," Mrs. Sutton said. "It's such an exciting place. I lived there for a summer after I graduated from college. I'd love to go back for a visit."

"Yeah, it's a great city," Ashley said. "But living in Sweet Valley must be like living in paradise. It's so incredibly beautiful."

"I think Sweet Valley is the prettiest place in the world," Mr. Sutton agreed. "And I know I speak for all of us when I say that we want you to come back here regularly for visits. Maybe you'd even consider spending a summer here."

Amy felt a little thrill as she imagined spending the summer hanging out at the beach with her sister. In fact, she liked the idea of hanging out with Ashley year-round. She was already feeling that she didn't want Ashley to leave.

"That sounds great," Ashley said.

"I can't wait to show you off at school tomorrow," Amy told her. "I just hope my classes won't be too boring—I mean, since you're in seventh grade and I'm only in sixth."

"Oh, I don't care about that," Ashley said with a shrug. "It will be fun just hanging out with you and meeting all your friends."

Mrs. Sutton glanced at her watch. "Speaking of school, it's time you two young ladies got yourselves into bed."

"It's supposed to get a little chilly tonight, sweetheart," Mr. Sutton said, carrying their empty mugs to the sink. "You should grab an extra blanket from the linen closet."

Thanks, Dad, Amy was about to say as she got up from the table. But when she looked up, the words died in her throat. Her dad was talking to Ashley, not to her. Amy looked down, feeling a flush creep over her cheeks.

"Thanks, Dad, I will," Ashley said.

There's no reason why Dad shouldn't call Ashley "sweetheart," too, Amy told herself.

"Good night," Ashley said, kissing Mr. Sutton on the cheek.

Amy's stomach felt strange again.

"Come on," Ashley said softly as they headed for the stairs. "We can stay up late if we're quiet. We still have so much left to talk about."

Amy giggled, and she felt her stomachache disappear. Having Ashley around was wonderful.

"Jessica! Let's go!" Elizabeth urged. It was Friday morning, and Elizabeth was standing impatiently in the doorway of Jessica's room.

Jessica didn't budge. She kept looking back and forth between her reflection in her mirror and her international hairstyling book.

"*Jessica!*" Elizabeth yelled. "I don't want to get another late mark in homeroom because of you and your dumb hairstyles."

"Relax, will you? I'm almost done." Jessica parted her hair in the back and started braiding. "This is a very complicated hairstyle. It requires a lot of attention." She bent over at the waist and flipped her hair upside-down.

"We're going to get a lot of attention from the principal today if we don't leave for school right this minute," Elizabeth said, knowing that her words wouldn't do any good. Jessica wouldn't cut short her primping for anything.

"OK, here it is," Jessica said, standing back up. She had woven her hair into two braids and criss-crossed them over the top of her head. "It's called a Swiss Heidi."

"Where's your cow?" Steven asked, poking his head into Jessica's room. "Is it lost with your sheep?" Steven was Elizabeth and Jessica's older brother. He was a freshman at Sweet Valley High, and his favorite activity, besides basketball, was teasing his sisters.

Elizabeth sighed and looked at her watch.

"Get out of my room, Steven!" Jessica shouted. "Nobody invited you to come in here."

Steven was laughing and pointing at Jessica's hair. "You're not seriously going to school like that, are you?"

"Yes, I am," Jessica said defensively. "What about it?"

"Jess, can't we go now?" Elizabeth pleaded. "Just ignore him."

"I'd be careful about leaving this house looking like that," Steven said, staring incredulously at Jessica's hair. "Someone might think you escaped from the Sweet Valley Mental Institution. They'll probably put you in a straitjacket and have you committed."

Jessica's mouth turned into an angry line. She grabbed a pillow from her bed and threw it at Steven. "I didn't ask for your stupid opinion in the first place!" she yelled as he went running down the hall.

Jessica looked at Elizabeth worriedly. "Tell me the truth, Elizabeth. What do you think of my hair?"

"It doesn't matter, because we don't have time for you to mess with it any longer," Elizabeth said, urgently. "We have to go! *Now!*"

"That means you hate it," Jessica said, looking back in the mirror. "I can't leave until I've taken my hair down."

Elizabeth groaned and marched out the door. Jessica could walk to school by herself. *Why do sisters have to be such a pain sometimes?* she wondered sourly.

"That's a really cool turtleneck," Ashley said to Amy on Friday morning as the two of them got ready for school in Amy's bedroom.

Amy had just pulled her new purple turtleneck out of her drawer. Amy had seen it at the mall earlier that week and had chosen it with Ashley in mind. She didn't wear a lot of purple, but she knew it was a fashionable color, and she had wanted her new sister to think she had good taste in clothes.

"Hey, I've got an idea. Why don't you wear it today?" Amy offered.

"Are you serious?" Ashley asked in disbelief. "That's so nice of you."

"That's what sisters do. They wear each other's clothes," Amy said, thinking about Elizabeth and Jessica and all their clothes-swapping.

"Wow! It looks great on you," Amy said, as Ashley tucked the shirt into her jeans. "It's almost like it was made for you." *In fact, it looks about a hundred times better on you than on me,* she couldn't help thinking. Ashley was a lot more developed than Amy was.

"Thanks," Ashley said, giving Amy a quick hug. "You're the best sister in the whole world!"

Four

"It looks like your sister's a big hit," Elizabeth said to Amy. It was Friday morning, and Jessica and Elizabeth were standing by Amy's locker between classes, waiting for Ashley to come out of the girls' bathroom. "About five guys have come up to me in the last five minutes to ask who the pretty new girl is."

"She's really cool," Jessica said. "I bet she's really popular at her school in New York."

"She is," Amy said, pulling a book from the top shelf of her locker. "She has a zillion boyfriends who are all gorgeous. She showed me pictures of them last night."

"She seems really sophisticated," Jessica added. "I guess that's because she's from New York City. I mean, talk about glamorous. After New York, Sweet Valley must seem like a total bore."

"Don't tell me you're bored, Jess. Don't the Unicorns have any exciting gossip these days?" Elizabeth teased. "Didn't one of you buy a new outfit you could talk about?"

"Very funny," Jessica retorted.

Elizabeth turned to Amy. "I can see why you were so excited about having Ashley here. She seems so nice."

"Yeah," Amy said in a small voice. "She's great."

Elizabeth studied her friend's face for a moment, feeling puzzled. Amy didn't look all that happy.

"You know, it's pretty hard to imagine that you two are really sisters," Jessica said.

Amy spun around to look at Jessica. "What do you mean?" she asked, looking slightly hurt.

"Well, you just seem so different," Jessica explained. "I guess that happens. I mean, look at me and Elizabeth. If we didn't look exactly alike, you'd never know we were sisters."

Amy's face turned hard. "Actually, it turns out that Ashley and I have a lot more in common than you might think. In fact, if you get to know Ashley better, it will be pretty obvious we're sisters." She slammed her locker door and took off down the hall.

"What's with her?" Jessica asked.

"I don't know," Elizabeth said, shaking her head. "I was just wondering the same thing myself."

"Hey, Ashley, we were wondering if you'd like

to sit with us in the Unicorner today," Lila asked as she approached Ashley and Amy in the lunch line.

I don't get it, Amy thought. *Ashley's only been in school a couple of hours, and she's already buddies with one of the most popular girls.* "Um, you've already met Lila, I guess," Amy mumbled, turning to Ashley.

"We met this morning in the girls' room," Ashley explained. "She told me all about the Unicorns, and I told her about the group I belong to in New York, called the Butterflies."

"You're even wearing the right color and everything," Lila said approvingly.

"What do you mean?" Ashley asked.

"Purple! The Unicorns try to wear something purple every day. That's a fabulous turtleneck," Lila said, moving her tray along the line.

"Thanks, but actually it's Amy's," Ashley said, smiling at her sister.

"I just got it at the mall," Amy added.

"So, Ashley," Lila continued, not even glancing at Amy, "are you coming to the Unicorner?"

"Well, that's really nice of you. What do you say, Amy?" Ashley smiled brightly.

Amy looked down at the floor. She knew that Lila's invitation didn't include her, and she didn't want to see the scornful look in Lila's eyes. "Actually, I wanted you to sit with me and Elizabeth at our usual table today. But do whatever you want."

"That really sounds thrilling," Lila said, rolling her eyes. "No offense, Amy, but she'll have a lot more fun in the Unicorner."

Amy felt her cheeks burning. *How could she embarrass me like that in front of Ashley?*

Ashley frowned a little. "Thanks anyway, Lila, but I'm going to sit with Amy and Elizabeth," she said.

"Well, have fun. I'm sure it will be a laugh a minute," Lila said as she walked away with her tray.

"Maybe you should sit with the Unicorns," Amy said as soon as Lila was out of hearing distance. "They are the most popular girls in the school. It's kind of an honor to be asked to eat with them."

Ashley shook her head. "I think it's a bigger honor to sit with my new sister."

"I bet you go to museums all the time in New York," Elizabeth said to Ashley between bites of spaghetti.

"Yeah, I do," Ashley said. "Our school takes a field trip to a different museum almost every month. The Metropolitan Museum is my favorite."

"I just read this great book about a brother and sister who hid in the Metropolitan Museum when they were closing it up at the end of the day. They slept there after everyone was gone," Elizabeth said.

"*From the Mixed-Up Files of Mrs. Basil E.*

Frankweiler!" Ashley exclaimed. "That's one of my favorite books of all time."

"Me, too," Elizabeth said excitedly.

"Have you read it, Amy?" Ashley asked.

Amy looked down at her plate of spaghetti. "Um, no," she muttered.

"I'll lend it to you," Elizabeth offered. "You'll really like it."

"Great," Amy said flatly.

Elizabeth touched Amy's sleeve. "Look who's heading this way."

"Who's that?" Ashley asked, looking up. "He's pretty cute."

"Bruce Patman," Elizabeth said. "He's a seventh-grader and one of the most obnoxious guys in school. He's totally stuck-up."

"Who's stuck-up?" Bruce asked as he approached the table.

"Um . . . uh . . ." Elizabeth sputtered.

"This guy who goes to my school in New York," Ashley filled in quickly.

Elizabeth slapped her hand over her mouth to keep herself from laughing. *Good save,* she thought, darting a quick glance at Ashley.

Bruce extended his hand to Ashley. "Hi, I'm Bruce. And you are . . . ?"

"I'm Ashley."

"She's my sister," Amy explained. "She's staying with me for two weeks."

Bruce's eyebrows shot up in surprise. "Well, I

hope we'll get a chance to get to know each other better while you're here," he said, running his fingers through his dark hair. "If you need a tour guide to show you the sights of Sweet Valley, let me know."

"That's nice of you, Bruce," Amy said, sitting up, "but Ashley already has a tour guide. Me."

"Well, if you get tired of the kiddie tour, let me know," Bruce said. He winked at Ashley, then walked away.

"He is pretty awful, isn't he?" Ashley said, giggling as she watched Bruce walk away.

"Totally," Elizabeth said.

"Too bad," Ashley said, sighing. "He's so darn cute."

"I'd stay away from him if I were you," Amy said.

"Don't worry, I will," Ashley said. "But who's *he*?"

Elizabeth turned her head and saw Denny Jacobson approaching their table.

"Hey, you must be Ashley," Denny said smoothly. "I've been wanting to introduce myself since I saw you in the hallway this morning."

Elizabeth watched Amy fiddling with the wrapper on her straw. Denny was also considered to be one of the cutest guys in the school.

"Nice to meet you," Ashley said, returning his gaze.

Amy put down her fork. "We *are* trying to eat our lunch here."

"Sorry," Denny said. He flashed a big smile at Ashley. "I'll see you around."

"Wow," Elizabeth said as Denny walked away. "Not even my sister attracts so much attention from guys."

Ashley waved her hand dismissively. "It's probably just because I'm a new face around here. By tomorrow, it'll wear off."

Elizabeth turned to Amy. "I think your sister's being modest, don't you?"

Amy was frowning as she picked nervously at her fingernail. "I really need to . . . finish my English homework," Amy said suddenly as she jumped up from the table. "I'm sure you guys have plenty of stuff to talk about without me."

Elizabeth felt a chill as she watched Amy walk off. *It looks like Amy's having a harder time with this sister thing than I'd even imagined.*

"That's Aaron Dallas sitting by the window. He's my sort-of boyfriend," Jessica whispered to Ashley during social studies class on Friday afternoon. Jessica and Ashley were sitting next to each other, and Amy and Elizabeth were right behind them.

"Shhhhhh," Elizabeth urged.

"Shhhhhh yourself," Jessica whispered back in an irritated voice.

"I'm just trying to keep you from getting in trouble," Elizabeth said.

Lizzie's such a goody-goody, Jessica thought, rolling her eyes at Ashley.

"Aaron's adorable," Ashley whispered. "Is he nice?"

"He's great," Jessica said.

"Jessica! Would you like to share whatever it is that's so interesting with the rest of the class?" Mrs. Arnette asked.

Jessica smiled brightly. "I was just telling Ashley about our homework assignment for last night," she lied.

"That's very helpful of you, Jessica, but please don't talk while I'm trying to conduct class," Mrs. Arnette said.

"Hairnet is always on my case," Jessica whispered to Ashley.

"Who's Hairnet?" Ashley asked.

"That's what we call Mrs. Arnette, because she wears that stupid hairnet every day."

Ashley and Jessica started to giggle.

"Shhhhh!" Elizabeth and Amy hissed at the same time.

"Our sisters are definitely the nerds of the family," Jessica said to Ashley. "And we're the fun ones."

"Amy's a lot of fun," Ashley whispered back.

"Yeah, about as much fun as sitting through this class," Jessica said, rolling her eyes.

"Jessica Wakefield!" Mrs. Arnette said sternly. "I don't want to have to ask you to be quiet again. Do I have your attention?"

Jessica nodded, looking at her attentively.

"Now, you all have an exciting assignment due Thursday after next," Mrs. Arnette continued. "I want everyone to write an essay about the person you admire the most and why you admire him or her."

"I'll write mine on Mrs. Arnette," Jessica whispered, giggling.

"Jessica!" Mrs. Arnette shouted.

"I'm going to write my essay about Johnny Buck," Jessica told Ashley, Amy, and Elizabeth after class. Johnny Buck was Jessica's favorite rock star. She had all his CDs and every article ever written about him.

Amy couldn't help letting out a little giggle. *How typical of Jessica to write about a rock star for a homework assignment.*

"I don't think that's what Mrs. Arnette had in mind," Elizabeth said.

"I don't care what she had in mind," Jessica said, flipping her hair. "That's who I admire the most."

"I love Johnny Buck, too," Ashley said. "He's totally gorgeous. I love every one of his songs."

"Are you going to write *your* essay about Johnny Buck?" Amy asked Ashley, hoping she would say no.

Ashley shook her head. She had a thoughtful look on her face. "I was actually thinking I might do my essay about Dad."

Amy felt as if someone had punched her in her stomach. "Oh," she mumbled softly. She couldn't think of anything else to say.

Ashley's known Dad for less than a week, she thought unhappily. What could she possibly write about him?

It isn't enough that Ashley is prettier and more popular than me, Amy found herself thinking as she walked numbly back to her locker. *She wants to be the best daughter, too.*

Five

"That was an awesome pirouette," Jessica told Ashley, her voice full of amazement. "You're practically a professional!"

It was Saturday morning, and Jessica and Ashley were taking ballet class together at the Sweet Valley Dance Studio.

"I wouldn't exactly say that," Ashley said with a laugh. "But I love ballet. I've been taking lessons since I was four years old. I don't know about turning professional. It might stop being fun if I start taking it too seriously."

"Attention, ladies!" Madame André, the ballet instructor, announced, clapping her hands. "I see that we have an exceptional dancer here today. Ashley, would you please show the class the routine we just went through. I want you to all pay close attention to her movements. Her line is exquisite."

Jessica watched in awe as Ashley leaped and twirled around the studio gracefully and effortlessly. "Bravo!" Madame André exclaimed. "That, my girls, is what ballet is supposed to be."

All the girls, including Jessica, applauded loudly. Normally, Jessica would have been jealous. If anyone was going to get a lot of attention, Jessica wanted it to be her. But Ashley wasn't at all like Lila, who'd go around bragging for the next six months if anyone paid her the smallest compliment. Ashley was totally nice and modest. Besides, Ashley would be leaving Sweet Valley soon, so she wasn't a real threat.

"That was *so* incredible," Jessica told Ashley as they walked to the dressing room after class. "I wish I could dance like that."

"You're a very talented dancer," Ashley said, wiping her forehead with a towel. "I was watching you earlier. You're definitely one of the best in the class."

"Thanks," Jessica said, standing very tall with her feet slightly turned out the way ballerinas always did. "That means a lot coming from you."

"I was noticing how pretty your hair looked while you were dancing," Ashley continued. "Can you show me how to make that kind of bun?"

Jessica felt the bun on top of her head. "Definitely. It would look beautiful. I could help fix your hair for you sometime. I'm becoming an expert at different hairstyles."

Ashley would be a great Unicorn, Jessica decided as she watched all the other ballet students gather around her new friend. *She's exactly what we need to liven things up. And she appreciates a great hairstyle when she sees one.*

"Check out that adorable dress in the window," Jessica said, pointing to one of the most expensive shops in the mall. "Let's stop in and take a look."

Jessica, Elizabeth, Ashley, and Amy had been walking around the Valley Mall for what felt like hours that afternoon. Amy was exhausted from all the shopping, and she was getting sick of watching Jessica fawn all over her sister. *I wish Ashley and I had gone shopping alone,* she thought grumpily.

"Aren't you getting tired of shopping?" Elizabeth asked. "I don't know if I can go into another store."

"Who do you think you're talking to, Elizabeth? I never get tired of shopping," Jessica said.

"Me neither," Ashley said. "I could shop for hours on end. What about you, Amy?"

"Well, I guess I like shopping in small doses, but I do get bored kind of quickly."

"You two will just have to be bored a few more minutes," Jessica said, linking her arm through Ashley's and walking into the store. "That dress is too gorgeous to walk by."

"You're right," Ashley agreed. "I bet it would look great on you, Jessica."

"That's just what I was thinking," Jessica said. "I have to try it on."

"I seriously doubt Mom would let you buy a new dress," Elizabeth said. "Especially from that place."

"Who said anything about buying it?" Jessica asked as she marched over to the dress hanging on a rack. "I just want to see what it looks like on me."

"I do that all the time in New York," Ashley said, as the girls followed Jessica back into a dressing room. "I like to go to stores even when I know I'm not going to buy anything. It's fun just to try things on."

"Doesn't that get frustrating?" Amy asked. "Don't you always want to buy it if it looks good?"

"Yes and no," Ashley said. "Sometimes it's fun just to pretend that it's mine. Shopping is probably my favorite activity after ballet."

"Speaking of ballet, you should have seen your sister in class today," Jessica said to Amy as she pulled the dress on over her head. "She was unbelievable. I've never seen Madame André get so excited about anything before."

Ashley laughed modestly. "It wasn't that big a deal. Amy, did you ever take ballet lessons?"

Amy played with the buckle on her backpack. "Yeah, I did for a little while, but it didn't really work out," she said. "Ballet isn't exactly my thing." *Because I was absolutely terrible at it*, she added silently.

"So how do I look?" Jessica asked as she struck a model pose.

"Ridiculous," Elizabeth teased. "That dress looks like a potato sack on you."

"I was just thinking the same thing," Amy said, trying to hold back a giggle.

"Why am I even bothering to ask you two?" Jessica asked. "Ashley, you're from New York. You know about fashion. What do *you* think?"

Ashley studied Jessica's outfit with a frown. "Actually, I think it looks better on the hanger than on you. It's just the way it's cut."

So there, Amy thought with secret pleasure. She was glad Ashley agreed with her and not Jessica.

Jessica scrutinized herself in the mirror. "I see what you mean," she said to Ashley. "It just isn't me."

"Hey, Amy, wasn't your grandmother a ballet dancer?" Elizabeth asked, feeling the velvety fabric of a skirt hanging on the dressing room wall. "I remember your dad telling us about her when we used to take ballet."

"Yeah, my dad talks about her all the time," Amy said. "She was a professional dancer. He has a scrapbook full of pictures of her in her dancing costumes and programs from her recitals." Amy thoughtfully twisted a button on her jacket. "I guess one of the reasons I used to take lessons was that he thought I might have inherited her talent." She laughed, suddenly embarrassed. "I guess it's safe to say I didn't, huh?"

"You didn't, but Ashley *definitely* inherited her talent," Jessica broke in as she put her clothes back on.

Amy felt her heart sink. She hadn't allowed herself to think about it before, but Jessica was absolutely right.

Ashley was a great ballerina, just like Grandma Sutton. Ashley had inherited all the talent in the family, and Amy had inherited none of it.

"Pass the fried chicken, would you?" Steven asked Jessica at dinner at the Wakefields' house that night.

"You've had four pieces already," Jessica pointed out. "Does the word *pig* mean anything to you?"

"That's not a nice thing to call your brother," Mr. Wakefield said.

"Well, he's eating like one," Jessica said.

"I'm a growing boy," Steven said, defending himself as he reached for a wing. "Besides, my brain is so enormous that it needs extra energy."

"Yeah, it's about as enormous as this pea on my spoon," Jessica said, holding up her spoon to demonstrate.

Elizabeth sighed. She was getting tired of hearing her brother and sister squabble. It happened all the time, but it bothered her more some days than others. "Did I tell you all what I'm writing my essay about for social studies class?" Elizabeth asked her family, trying to come up with something to talk about besides how much Steven ate.

"No, you didn't, and I'm sure we're all dying to know," Steven said sarcastically.

"Steven, that's enough," Mrs. Wakefield said sternly. "Tell us what you're writing about, honey."

"The assignment is to write about the person you admire the most and why," Elizabeth said.

"And you're going to write about me," Steven said. "That's so sweet of you. I'm moved to tears."

"Right," Jessica said. "She's writing about how she admires the fact that you can consume more food than any other person in the world. She's comparing and contrasting you to a trash compactor."

"Elizabeth, would you like your father and me to send your brother and sister away from the table so the three of us can have a normal conversation?" Mrs. Wakefield asked.

"Yes, as a matter of fact, I would," Elizabeth said, smiling at Jessica and Steven.

"We'll be quiet, I swear," Steven promised. "I haven't eaten enough fried chicken yet. We trash compactors never leave a dinner table that still has food left on it."

Mr. Wakefield shot a warning look at Steven. "Who are you writing about, Elizabeth?" he asked.

"I'm writing about our new First Lady," Elizabeth answered.

"That's wonderful," Mrs. Wakefield said. "She's an interesting and powerful woman. I think she's a good role model for young people. Especially young girls."

"Did I tell you about the book I've been reading that's all about international hairstyles?" Jessica asked her parents.

Elizabeth rolled her eyes. She was even more tired of hearing about Jessica's hairstyles than she was of listening to her siblings argue.

"Did you say *reading*?" Steven asked, pretending to be shocked. "When did you learn how to do that?"

So much for my essay, Elizabeth thought, as Jessica and Steven started bickering once again. *This is one of those moments when I think it wouldn't be so bad to be an only child!*

"You're so lucky to have a pool in your back-yard. Especially one you can swim in all year round," Ashley said, adjusting the strap of her bright-turquoise bikini. She and Amy were spending their Sunday afternoon hanging out by the Wakefields' pool. "I never go swimming in New York."

"It is pretty awesome," Jessica said, rubbing suntan lotion on her arms. "I can stay tan all year."

"And you can work on getting premature wrinkles all year," Elizabeth said.

"You sound like Mom," Jessica said. "Lighten up, Elizabeth."

"Are the winters in New York as horrible as

people say?" Amy asked. She was feeling babyish and awkward in her one-piece bathing suit.

"Last winter was the worst," Ashley said. "One week it snowed twenty inches. The cars were totally buried under the snow."

"I bet it was great to get out of school, though," Jessica said.

"Yeah, well, when it snows in New York City, the schools sometimes stay open," Ashley said. "It's not like in the suburbs."

"I'd think it would be fun to have all that snow around to play in," Amy said.

"It is at first, but then it all turns this disgusting blackish-gray color," Ashley said, scrunching up her face.

"Hey, kiddies," Steven said, walking through the glass doors and onto the patio. When he saw Ashley he did a double take. "Hi. I don't think we've met before."

"This is Amy's half sister, Ashley," Elizabeth said. "She's visiting Sweet Valley for a little while."

Steven's eyes opened wide. "Hi, Ashley." He smiled at her. "It's an honor to have you here at our humble abode."

"Yuck, stop flirting," Jessica said. "You're making me nauseous."

"Nice to meet you," Ashley said. "What's your name?"

"Steven," Jessica said. "We usually keep him

locked up in his bedroom. We let him out for feeding times."

"You can see that my sisters are very mature," Steven said to Ashley.

"I think I hear *Cathy* calling you," Elizabeth said pointedly.

"Yeah, Steven," Jessica added. "What would your girlfriend say if she knew what a flirt you were?"

Steven shot her a withering glare. "It was great meeting you," he said to Ashley. "I'll see you around."

"Unfortunately for you, our goofy brother has a crush on you," Jessica said as soon as Steven was back inside the house. "I'd stay away from him if I were you."

Ashley was blushing. "He's very good-looking," she said. "I have a weakness for tall, dark types."

Amy's face burned. She secretly thought Steven was cute, too, but it didn't matter. He would never even notice she existed. He, along with practically every other male in Sweet Valley, was going nuts over her sister. It was bad enough when it was just the middle school, but now Ashley had captured the attention of a cute high-school guy. What was next?

Six

$\Diamond$

"Who can tell us what ions are?" Mr. Seigel asked his science class on Monday morning. "How about you, Amy?"

Amy looked up at Mr. Seigel. She remembered reading about ions the night before, but she couldn't remember well enough to explain what they were. She was a good student in all her other subjects, but sometimes she had trouble in science. "I'm . . . um . . . not exactly sure. . . ."

"Anybody else want to try?" Mr. Seigel asked, scanning around the room. "Ashley? What about you? Can you explain what ions are?"

Ashley looked completely calm in spite of the fact that the entire class was staring at her. "I'm pretty sure an ion is an electrically charged particle or group of atoms," Ashley answered. She looked over at Amy and shrugged. Amy forced a smile back.

"Very impressive," Mr. Seigel said. "Maybe you could help your sister with this material while you're visiting Sweet Valley."

Amy wanted to sink into the floor. *Does Ashley have to be better than me at everything?*

"You seem like you're really good at science," Amy said to Ashley as soon as class ended. "It's my worst subject."

"Actually, I'm not that great in science," Ashley said. "It's just that I'm a year ahead of you in school, so I learned this stuff last year."

"Oh, yeah. That's right," Amy said, starting to feel better. "Maybe you *could* help me with my science homework."

"I'd love to," Ashley said. "And maybe you could help me learn how to write a newspaper article."

"It's a deal," Amy said, feeling happier than she had all day.

"It's so cool to have a sister who's a writer," Ashley went on. "I have such a hard time stringing ideas together. It's a miracle that I've actually been able to write this essay on Dad. It's really coming along great—probably because the subject's so great. I'm so glad I'm getting to know him better."

Amy's good mood clouded over. This was too much. She couldn't stand to hear Ashley acting as if she were some kind of authority on their father.

"By the way," Ashley said brightly, "how's

your essay on Martin Luther King going?"

As she glanced at her sister's beautiful, smiling face, Amy suddenly had an idea. "Actually, I changed my mind. It's not on Martin Luther King anymore. It's on Dad."

Ashley looked a little perplexed, but Amy walked to class triumphantly, proud of her inspiration. There was no way Ashley would be able to write a better essay about their father than she could. Not only was Amy a good writer, but she'd known him her whole life. *Finally, I'll be better at something than Ashley!*

"What's with the hair?" Lila asked Jessica, obviously suppressing a giggle. They were sitting at the Unicorner on Monday along with the rest of the Unicorn Club. "You look like you're stuck in the fifties or sixties or something. Isn't that what they call a beehive?"

"It's an Italian Basilica," Jessica said, straightening her hair on top. "It's actually all the rage in Italy."

"Well, no offense, but I don't really see it catching on in Sweet Valley," Lila said, the corners of her mouth twitching.

Everyone at the table except Jessica burst into giggles.

"I guess you just have to have sophisticated taste to appreciate the look," Jessica said haughtily.

Janet sighed as she plunked a container of

yogurt on the table. "I can't believe we're talking about Jessica's hair again," she complained. "Doesn't anyone have any good gossip?"

Ellen pointed her spoon at Jessica. "Hey, whatever happened to that idea about finding a new Unicorn?" she asked.

"Let's face it, there's really nobody out there who meets our standards," Lila said.

"You're so wrong, Lila," Jessica said. "I know the perfect Unicorn. She's pretty, popular, talented, and nice—and she loves Johnny Buck."

"Who are you talking about?" Tamara asked. "Are you sure this person goes to our school?"

"She doesn't go to our school. She's just visiting for a while," Jessica said. "She could be a temporary member."

"Ashley!" the Unicorns all said in unison.

"You guessed it," Jessica said.

"I think that's a great idea, Jessica," Janet said approvingly. "She seems like great Unicorn material."

"She was telling me that she's a member of a group that sounds a lot like the Unicorns at her school in New York," Jessica said.

"And I hear she's a great ballet dancer," Mandy Miller said. "Some girls who were in her class on Saturday said she was awesome."

"She was," Jessica said. "She's practically a professional dancer."

Lila cleared her throat. "I'm not saying that Ashley *wouldn't* be a good Unicorn, but I think we're forgetting that we really don't know her very well. I think we should all get to know her a little bit better before we let her join. After all, it *is* a privilege to be a Unicorn. It's not like we can just invite any old stranger to spend time with us."

"But it's just for a little while," Jessica said. "She's only here for a couple of weeks. And I can guarantee that she's a very cool girl."

Janet held up her hand. "Lila has a point. Let's give her a chance to prove her Unicorn credentials, and then we'll decide."

Jessica shot Lila a quick glare. *Leave it to Lila to make everything more complicated than it has to be. She's just being a pain about letting Ashley join because I suggested it.*

"So how is everyone going to decide?" Jessica asked.

"I'll call Ashley tonight and invite her to do something with us," Janet said. "We'll spend a little time with her, and then we'll take a vote."

"Speaking of voting," Jessica said, running a hand through her heavily sprayed hair, "everyone who likes my hair this way raise their right hand."

She looked around the table and realized that the only raised arm was her own. "Oh, fine. I get the message," Jessica said as she started to take the hairpins out of her hair.

"It's about time," Lila said. "I was starting to worry that that beehive was going to scare people away!"

* * *

"Shoot! I just can't seem to get this new kick right," Amy complained. She was at Booster practice on Tuesday afternoon, and she'd been trying for almost an hour to do the new routine. The Boosters were the cheering and baton squad for Sweet Valley Middle School, and every single Booster except for Amy and Winston Egbert was also a Unicorn.

"Try being a little more graceful as you lift your leg," Janet instructed Amy. "Here. Watch me." Janet went through the routine and ended with a perfect kick to the front.

Amy attempted the same routine, but her leg landed with a thud on the floor. *If everyone would just stop watching me, I'd be able to do this,* Amy thought as she pulled down the sleeves of her leotard.

"Try imagining that you're a butterfly," Jessica suggested as she demonstrated her version of the spin, leap, and kick. "You want to be light and airy."

"OK, I'll try that," Amy said. She wished everyone would just leave her alone.

Amy took a deep breath and began the sequence again, but this time each of her steps made an echoing thud.

"Don't worry," Tamara said. "It takes a while to learn a new routine."

"Thanks," Amy said, happy to have a word of sympathy.

"Yeah, not everyone can be graceful," Ellen said with a snicker.

Get me out of here, Amy thought, dropping her baton and heading to the bleachers, where the Boosters were gathering up their belongings. *This has to be the worst practice of all time.*

"Hey, Amy, can you write down your phone number for me?" Janet asked.

Amy turned around and stared at Janet in shock. *Janet Howell actually wants my phone number! This day's starting to get better.* "Sure, Janet, no problem," she said excitedly. She scribbled down her number on a piece of notebook paper and handed it to Janet.

"Great. Thanks," Janet said.

As Amy bounded out of the gym, she felt as though she were floating on air. *Maybe they want to ask me to be a Unicorn*, she thought hopefully. *Then Ashley would really be impressed.*

"I hate that guy," Ashley squealed. "He's a total idiot. I can't stand that moronic bow tie he's always wearing."

"Yeah, really," Amy said, laughing. "I usually flip the channel during the parts that he's on."

It was Tuesday night, and Amy and Ashley were in the Suttons' family room watching TV. They'd been laughing together all night. *She's not just a sister, she's a great friend*, Amy thought, as she watched Ashley tuck her feet under herself on the couch. *I can't believe I've been so jealous of her lately.*

"Hey, you know, you look like that actress, Bonnie Bartlett, who's on this show sometimes. Did anyone ever tell you that?" Ashley asked.

"No way!" Amy said, both thrilled and shocked.

"I'm serious, you look a lot like her."

"Oh, come on. She's about a hundred million times prettier than me," Amy said.

"That's not true at all. You're just as pretty as she is, if not prettier," Ashley said.

Amy waved her hand dismissively. "You're the pretty one."

"*Me?* You're beautiful," Ashley said. "I can't believe you don't know that."

Amy picked up a limp strand of hair. "Look," Amy said. "It just hangs there like a rag. I wish I had wavy hair like you do."

Ashley's eyes lit up. "I know a way to make your hair wavy."

"My mom won't let me get a perm," Amy said. "I've already asked. She says I'm too young."

"There's a way to make it wavy without giving you a perm," Ashley said. "Come sit on the floor in front of me."

Amy did as she was told.

"Wait a second," Ashley said. She jumped up from the couch and came back a few moments later with a brush and a towel. "I soaked the brush with water," Ashley explained, running it through Amy's fine hair. "It works better if your hair's a little damp." Ashley started to braid Amy's hair quickly and expertly in lots of individual sections. "You're going to sleep with your hair in these braids. Then when you wake up in the morning, your hair will be super-wavy. When we go upstairs, I'll tie holders around the bottoms to keep them secure during the night."

"Wow, you're a genius," Amy said. "Do you really think this will work?"

"Definitely," Ashley said.

"I can't wait to see how it turns out," Amy said excitedly.

Just then, the phone rang.

"Hang on a second, I'll get it," Amy said. She walked across the room, holding on to the bottoms of her braids. "Hello."

"Hi, Amy, it's Janet."

Janet Howell is actually calling me! Amy thought with a flutter of excitement in her stomach. *An eighth grader and the president of the Unicorns is calling me!*

"Hi!" Amy practically yelled into the phone. "How are you?"

"Fine," Janet answered.

"You were great in practice today," Amy gushed.

"Thanks," Janet said. "Listen, I was actually calling to talk to Ashley. Is she there?"

"To Ashley?" Amy repeated, her heart sinking. She dropped her arm limply to her side. "Ashley, it's Janet Howell for you." Amy handed Ashley the receiver, then plopped down on the couch, listening to Ashley's end of the conversation.

"Hi, Janet. Amy and I were just watching *Star Watch*. . . . Yeah, it's pretty funny. . . . Tomorrow? . . . What's Casey's? . . . I'd love to, and I'm sure Amy would, too. . . . So I can bring her? . . . Great. I'll see you tomorrow. Bye."

"Janet just invited you and me to go to Casey's tomorrow afternoon with the Unicorns," Ashley said, plunking herself back down onto the couch. "Won't that be fun?"

"Yeah, that sounds great," Amy said, forcing a smile. She knew perfectly well the only reason Janet had invited her was that Ashley had asked her to.

I should have known that Janet really just wanted my number so she could talk to my sister, Amy thought miserably, trying not to let herself cry. *Ashley's been here for less than a week, and already she's more popular than I'll ever be in my entire life.*

Seven

"These are some of the best blueberry pancakes I've ever had," Mr. Sutton said to Ashley on Wednesday morning. Ashley had woken up extra early to make pancakes, and the Suttons were gathered around the kitchen table eating them.

"Actually, you know who used to make delicious blueberry pancakes?" Mrs. Sutton asked.

"My mother," Mr. Sutton said, smiling. "She made them all the time when I was a little boy."

"And then she used to make them whenever she came to visit us after we were married," Mrs. Sutton said.

"I never thought I'd taste such fabulous pancakes again. But these are just as good. I see you've inherited her talent. You're a great cook, Ashley," Mr. Sutton said.

"Thanks, Dad," Ashley said. She sighed contentedly. "My whole life I've been wanting to say that word. It feels great to finally be able to say it."

It may feel great to say it, but it still feels weird to hear it, Amy thought. She pushed away her plate. The pancakes *were* delicious, but she suddenly couldn't eat another bite.

"I just wish we'd been together earlier in your life," Mr. Sutton said, covering Ashley's hand with his own. "But you're here now, and that's what matters."

Amy squirmed in her seat as she watched all the bonding going on at the table. "So do you cook a lot?" she asked Ashley, quickly changing the subject.

"All the time," Ashley replied. "I love cooking. What about you?"

Mr. and Mrs. Sutton started laughing. "Amy can barely boil water for pasta," Mr. Sutton teased. "Cooking is not one of her talents."

Amy's face turned hot. *He's only joking*, she told herself, but it didn't make her feel any better. It was obvious that Ashley was better at everything than she was.

"Hey, maybe you and I can cook something together," Ashley suggested to Amy. "It's really pretty easy once you learn the basics."

Amy pushed a strand of hair behind her ear. "I doubt I'd be very good at it," she mumbled.

"Oh, come on," Ashley said encouragingly. "It's a lot easier than you might think."

Amy sighed listlessly. "OK, maybe sometime."

"Meanwhile, I'm going to have more of these fabulous pancakes," Mr. Sutton said, loading up his plate.

"That's Ken with the blue-and-white striped T-shirt," Amy whispered to Ashley during math class on Wednesday afternoon. "He's the one I told you was my sort-of boyfriend."

"The one throwing spitballs?" Ashley asked.

"Yeah, and the person he's throwing them at is my sort-of boyfriend, Todd Wilkins," Elizabeth said, rolling her eyes. "You can see that they're very mature."

Why can't Ken act normal for one second? Amy wondered. She wanted Ashley to be impressed that she had a boyfriend. But throwing spitballs didn't make him look all that impressive.

"He looks cute," Ashley said.

"He doesn't usually act like that," Amy explained quickly.

"Yes, he does," Elizabeth said, laughing. "Those two are always throwing spitballs and erasers at each other."

Can't you just keep your mouth shut, Elizabeth? Amy wanted to say to her friend. Why did Elizabeth always have to be so honest?

Just then Caroline Pearce, the biggest gossip in the school, leaned over and handed Ashley a note. "Rick Hunter wanted me to give this to you," she whispered.

"What does it say?" Amy asked Ashley.

"'You have a beautiful smile,'" Ashley read from the note, her cheeks turning pink. "Which one is Rick?"

"He's sitting in the front row, wearing a light-blue shirt," Elizabeth said.

"He also happens to be one of the cutest and most popular guys in the school," Caroline said. "You're so lucky. Most girls would kill to have Rick send them a note."

"Did Ashley ask your opinion?" Amy snapped, surprising herself at the tone of her own voice. "Maybe you should mind your own business for a change."

"I think somebody woke up on the wrong side of the bed," Caroline said. "Or maybe somebody's just jealous of all the attention *their sister's* getting," she hissed before she turned away.

Amy was burning up with fury and embarrassment. She turned abruptly to Ashley. "I wouldn't pay any attention to anything Caroline says to you. She's a total busybody."

"I'll remember that," Ashley said.

"And don't tell her anything you don't want the whole school to know," Amy continued hotly. "She has the biggest mouth in California."

"Thanks for the advice," Ashley said, looking a tiny bit embarrassed.

Amy had a hard time regaining her breath once she had finished ranting against Caroline. And she couldn't tell Ashley what was *really* bothering her. The problem wasn't that Caroline would spread rumors about Rick and Ashley—it was what she'd said about Amy's jealousy.

Caroline spread a lot of phony rumors, but this time what she was saying was absolutely true.

"We're lucky we're allowed in this place," Jessica told Ashley at Casey's on Wednesday afternoon. "Casey was kind of mad at me and Janet about a little food-fighting incident that happened a couple of weeks ago."

"Well, I'm glad he got over it," Ashley said, picking up her cherry. "This sundae is delicious."

"Yeah, this is the best ice cream in Sweet Valley," Amy said enthusiastically, looking around at the Unicorns crowded in the booth. "And by the way, Janet, I really like your shirt. It looks great on you."

"Thanks," Janet said unenthusiastically.

"Where'd you get it?" Amy asked.

Janet looked at Amy as if she had just asked the dumbest question in the world. "I bought it at a store."

Amy was feeling awkward and invisible. Every time she tried to make a joke or say something, everyone ignored her—everyone except for Ashley.

"Amy's doing this really cool article for the *Sixers*," Ashley told the Unicorns. "Amy, tell them what it's about."

"Well—" Amy began.

"No offense, Amy, but I think we'd all rather hear more about your sister's life in New York," Lila said as she scooped up a spoonful of whipped cream. "I mean, I'm sure your article's really fascinating and all, but we can read it when it comes out in the paper."

"Sure," Amy muttered, staring down at her sundae. *It's nice of Ashley to try to include me,* she thought. But it was obvious Ashley was just feeling sorry for her. *And no wonder. The Unicorns don't even really want me here—they just want to hang out with my sister.*

"So anyway, I'm dying to know about the stores in New York," Grace Oliver said excitedly. "You have the most amazing clothes. Do you shop at those huge department stores?"

"Actually, I get most of my clothes in the smaller boutiques in Greenwich Village," Ashley said. "The stuff is more interesting there."

"Wow, Greenwich Village just sounds so cool," Tamara said. "That's where I want to live someday."

"Yeah, it's a pretty great area," Ashley said. "The people there are so funky. Some of them are pretty shocking."

"What do you mean?" Ellen asked.

"People with earrings in their noses and purple hair. Stuff like that," Ashley said.

"I wish we had interesting people in Sweet Valley to look at," Jessica said.

"Well, since you've been so into changing your

hairstyle lately, you could just dye your hair purple," Lila teased. "It would be perfect, since that's the Unicorns' color."

Everyone laughed hysterically except for Amy, who felt completely out of it. *They just think they're the coolest people in the world,* she thought sourly. *Elizabeth's right. They're pretty silly.*

"Maybe I could start a new trend," Jessica said between giggles. "It'll look so cool that everyone in Sweet Valley will dye their hair purple."

"I'm sure our parents and teachers would really go for that," Mandy said.

"Can you imagine Hairnet's reaction if we all walked into social studies class with purple hair?" Ellen asked.

"While you're at it, you could pierce your noses," Ashley said, setting off more giggles around the table.

"And you could get Mohawks," Amy said, trying to join in on the joking.

Suddenly the table was silent. Except for Ashley, who politely laughed a little. Amy wanted to crawl under the table.

"Speaking of hair," Ashley said, smiling at Amy. "Don't you all think Amy's hair looks great all wavy like that?"

The Unicorns glanced at Amy for one second. "Sure," Jessica muttered.

Janet turned back to Ashley. "So do you ride the subways in New York?"

"Only in the daytime," Ashley said. "My mom won't let me ride them at night."

"Don't you get scared?" Lila asked, her eyes widening. "I've heard the subways there are really dangerous."

"They're not too bad," Ashley said, eating a spoonful of her banana split. "They're so crowded in the daytime that no one really bothers you."

Amy could easily picture Ashley acting cool and sophisticated as she shopped in Greenwich Village and rode the subways. *But I would never be like that in a million years.*

"Your sister and her friends are really great," Ashley said to Elizabeth on Thursday morning. Ashley and Amy were standing at Elizabeth's locker after homeroom.

"Yeah, Jessica's the greatest, but I'm not crazy about her friends," Elizabeth said.

"I had a lot of fun with them yesterday at Casey's. The Unicorns remind me of the club I belong to in New York called the Butterflies," Ashley said.

"You mean, you guys just sit around and talk about boys and clothes like the Unicorns?" Amy asked.

"Yeah, we talk about that stuff, but we also do volunteer work together," Ashley explained. "Like on Thursday afternoons we serve food at a homeless shelter."

"I'd like to see Lila and Janet at a homeless shelter," Elizabeth said with a laugh.

"Like that would ever happen," Amy said. "I think the Unicorns are such a bore. All they talked about yesterday at Casey's was hair and clothes."

"I thought you were having fun yesterday," Ashley said, her eyes clouding over. "I'm sorry you had a bad time."

Amy shrugged dismissively. "I guess the Unicorns just aren't my cup of tea."

"But last week you said you—" Elizabeth started. She stopped herself when she saw that Amy was turning bright red.

Keep your mouth shut, Elizabeth told herself. What was she thinking? Of course Amy didn't want Ashley to know that she was trying to impress her by becoming a Unicorn.

"What about last week?" Ashley asked.

"Oh . . . um," Amy began, obviously flustered. "Oh, whatever. Last week I told Elizabeth I wanted to be a Unicorn, but I've changed my mind, OK?"

Elizabeth and Ashley shared a confused glance as Amy strode away.

"Is she upset about something?" Ashley asked, looking genuinely concerned.

Elizabeth sighed. "I wish I knew."

Eight

◇

"What's that you're working on?" Mr. Sutton asked Amy, peering over the desk in his study on Thursday night.

"It's an essay for social studies class," Amy answered, covering her paper with her elbow. Since she'd decided to write her essay about her father, she thought it would be a good idea to observe him while he worked.

"What's it about?" he asked, settling back onto the couch, where he had been reading the newspaper.

"That's a secret," Amy said, smiling.

"Well, it's nice to have you here in my study with me," Mr. Sutton said. "How do you like having a sister around?"

"I love it," Amy said. She meant it, too. She really loved Ashley. She just wished she could stop feeling so jealous of her all the time. "She's really great. I'm really lucky that she's my sister."

"And I'm really lucky to have two wonderful daughters," Mr. Sutton said. He studied Amy's face for a moment. "I know it's an adjustment to get used to the fact that you have a sister, honey. I was worried that it might be hard for you. I'm so glad you're happy about it."

How could I ever have doubted that Dad would still love me even though he had another daughter? Amy wondered. *I've been acting so dumb lately.*

"I love you, Dad," Amy said.

"I love you, too, honey," Mr. Sutton said, getting up and kissing Amy on the forehead.

"Hey, guess what?" Ashley asked breathlessly as she sailed into the study.

"What is it?" Amy asked. "Is everything OK?"

Ashley's eyes were sparkling. "Everything is absolutely fantastic! Madame André just called. She wants me to dance the lead in *Sleeping Beauty*! The girl who was supposed to dance has the chicken pox, so they need a replacement. Can you believe that?"

"Ashley! Honey, this is incredible news! I'm so proud of you." Mr. Sutton wrapped his arms around Ashley and gave her a big hug.

"Amy, isn't this wonderful?" Mr. Sutton asked, turning to his other daughter.

"Yes, it is," Amy said, forcing a smile. "Congratulations, Ashley. I'm so happy for you." *I*

am happy for her. So why do I feel so crummy? She felt
as if she were two people—one person who loved
and was proud of her sister and another person
who was jealous and resentful.

"Your grandmother would be so proud of you if
she were alive," Mr. Sutton said. "Let me show you
the scrapbooks of all her dancing years."

"I'd love to see them," Ashley said enthusiastically.

Amy felt a lump in her throat. She couldn't bear
to be in the room with them one more minute. She
was afraid she might burst into tears.

"Excuse me," Amy almost whispered. "I have to
go see about something." Amy ran out of the study
and up to her room, where she collapsed facedown
on her bed and cried.

"So I hear that Rick Hunter has a crush on you,"
Jessica told Ashley on Friday as the two of them sat
down at the Unicorner. "He's a total catch."

"He seems like a nice guy," Ashley said. "But to
tell you the truth, I have enough boyfriends back
home to keep me busy."

"I can't believe your sister actually allowed you
to eat lunch with us today," Lila said. "I didn't
think you'd ever sit with us."

"She and Elizabeth are off doing something for
the *Sixers*," Ashley explained. "Amy's really a great
journalist."

"So I hear you're dancing the lead in the ballet

recital next week," Janet said. "That's really cool."

"I'm totally excited about it," Ashley said. "But I have to admit, I'm a little nervous, too."

"You'll be great," Jessica said. "You're an amazing dancer."

"Thanks," Ashley said. "I hope I won't disappoint Madame André."

Janet looked at Ashley with a serious expression. "Ashley, we have something important we want to talk to you about. We've decided that we'd like to make you an honorary Unicorn for the last week you're in Sweet Valley. And then every time you're back in town, you'll be an automatic member. We've all discussed it, and we think you're perfect Unicorn material."

"You forgot to mention that it was my idea," Jessica pointed out.

"What difference does it make?" Lila asked.

You know if it was your idea, you'd want credit for it, Jessica wanted to say. "Never mind," she said instead.

"Well, I'm really, really honored by the invitation," Ashley said. "I don't know what to say. Thanks for suggesting me, Jessica."

"You're welcome," Jessica said, making a face at Lila.

"So what do you think?" Ellen asked. "Are you going to join the ranks of the most popular girls in Sweet Valley?"

"It sounds like a great idea," Ashley said. "But

I'm going to have to think it over and talk to Amy about it."

What's there to think about? Jessica wondered. *And why would Amy have anything important to say about it? Maybe Ashley doesn't understand just how boring her sister is.*

"You think about it and get back to us as soon as you've made your decision," Janet said.

"It's a deal," Ashley said.

"Did I tell you my new story idea?" Elizabeth asked Amy in the *Sixers* office on Friday afternoon.

"We just finished this week's issue," Amy said. "I'm not ready to think about next week yet."

"I think you're going to like this one," Elizabeth said. "It's about someone who's really special to you."

"You're doing a story about Ken Matthews?"

Elizabeth laughed. "Why not? I could write about how he's the spitball champion of the school."

"Don't forget to include Todd in the article. He's right up there with the best of the spitballers," Amy joked.

"Seriously, I'm doing a story about your sister and how she's dancing the lead in the ballet," Elizabeth said. "People are always interested in visitors to the school. I thought I'd do an interview with her about her life in New York. What do you think?"

"Terrific," Amy muttered.

Elizabeth frowned. "What's wrong? Don't you like the idea?"

"I said I thought it was terrific. Now, can we not talk about it anymore?" Amy shuffled through some papers on the desk without looking up.

"Maybe you'd like to write the story yourself," Elizabeth suggested. "I'm so dumb. I should have thought of that in the first place. It makes total sense for you to write it. She's your sister, after all."

Amy slammed down her notebook on the desk. "I don't want to write it, and I don't want to have anything to do with it."

Elizabeth slid her chair back from the table in amazement. "Amy, I really don't have to do the story if you don't want me to."

"I don't care if you do the story. Just don't ask me to help."

Elizabeth sat down next to her friend. "Amy, what's going on with you?" she asked gently. "You've been acting strange ever since Ashley arrived."

Amy lifted her eyes. "Can I ask you a question?"

"Of course. You can ask me anything."

"Do you ever get jealous of Jessica?"

Elizabeth suddenly understood everything. "So that's what this is about—you're jealous of Ashley. I can't believe I've been so dense. I'm sorry I said all that stuff about the story."

"You have nothing to be sorry for," Amy said,

letting out a huge breath. "Besides, it's not exactly that I'm jealous."

"Are you sure about that?"

Amy sighed heavily. "Ashley's been so sweet and wonderful to me, and I really do love her. I'm so glad she's my sister and that she's here in Sweet Valley, but . . ."

"But you just wish she weren't quite so beautiful and talented and popular," Elizabeth concluded.

"Exactly. Do you think I'm a horrible person?" Amy asked meekly.

"No, I think you're a normal person. It's hard enough to find out one day that you have a sister out of the blue and even harder to find out that she's so terrific."

"So what about you and Jessica? Do you feel badly that she's so popular with the guys and that she's a Unicorn and everything?"

"I guess I sometimes get a little jealous, but not very often. There are some things that she's better at than I am, and there are some things I'm better at than she is. Like, Jessica couldn't write a newspaper article to save her life."

"Neither could Ashley," Amy said.

"Remember that time when you and I were still taking ballet classes and I was supposed to dance the lead? Well, in the end, I realized that it was Jessica who was the real ballet dancer in the family."

"That's right," Amy said. "And you even arranged it so that Jessica ended up dancing the lead after all. You told her you twisted your ankle, so that she would dance in your place."

"Right. You just have to accept that you and Ashley are different. Ashley's a pretty girl, but so are you, and you're each talented at different things. It's not as if you want to be a ballet dancer or anything."

"That's the truth," Amy said, smiling. "I like running shorts better than tutus anyway. I guess we're different, and that's OK."

"Just like me and Jessica. We're total opposites, but I love her more than anything in the world. And that doesn't mean she doesn't get on my nerves. You know she does—she and her silly hair-styles. But that's just part of having a sister. They're supposed to get on your nerves."

"You know, it's funny, but you and I seem pretty similar, and Jessica and Ashley seem a lot alike," Amy said.

"That's right," Elizabeth said. "And by the way, I'm really glad you changed your mind about join-ing the Unicorns. I thought I was going to lose my best friend for a while there."

"That will never happen," Amy assured her.

Nine

◇

"How's your essay going?" Ashley asked Amy on Saturday morning. They were sitting at the kitchen table after breakfast, working on their essays for social studies class.

"Oh, it's fine," Amy said, shuffling her papers. Actually, her essay wasn't going as well as she had hoped, but she didn't want Ashley to know that. For someone who hadn't had much practice as a writer, Ashley was certainly writing her essay at lightning speed. And she kept putting her hand over her notebook so that Amy couldn't see what she was writing. Amy was starting to get annoyed.

"You seem to have a lot to say," Amy said, watching Ashley fill up page after page.

"Yeah, I guess I do," Ashley said. "I'm really getting into this. I think it was a great assignment."

How could Ashley have so much more to say about Dad than I do? Amy wondered. *After all, I've known him my whole life, and she's only known him for a week.*

Amy tried to remind herself of what Elizabeth had said the day before—it was normal for Ashley to be better at some things, while Amy was better at others. But she couldn't push her competitive feelings away. After all, writing an essay about their father was one thing that Amy should be better at.

"Do you want some lemonade?" Ashley asked as she got up from the table.

"That would be great," Amy answered. *She's actually leaving her notebook open on the table*, she thought. As Ashley opened the refrigerator, Amy tried to crane her neck so that she could read from Ashley's notebook. Just as she was in a position where she would be able to see, Ashley turned back around.

This is getting ridiculous, Amy thought, sitting back. *I'm spying on my own sister.*

"You were great in rehearsal today," Jessica told Ashley on Saturday afternoon. They had just finished rehearsing *Sleeping Beauty* at the Sweet Valley Dance Studio and were doing some stretches at the barre. "I think this recital's really going to be terrific."

"I think so, too," Ashley said. "All of you girls

are really great dancers, and I think Madame André is a talented teacher."

"Yeah, she's tough but great," Jessica said. She didn't really mind how tough Madame André was—what was important was that she took Jessica seriously as a dancer.

"You should see my teacher in New York," Ashley said, laughing. "Talk about tough—she makes Madame André look like Mother Goose!"

Jessica giggled. "I guess everything is tougher in New York, huh? I bet you have to be super-gorgeous and talented and popular to be a Butterfly."

"Well, the Butterflies *are* pretty amazing," Ashley admitted. "A couple of them are great musicians. But mostly they're just really nice."

"So becoming a Unicorn wouldn't be such a huge step down or anything?" Jessica probed, smiling mischievously.

Ashley came up from a *plié* and looked at Jessica with a serious expression. "No way. I'd totally love to be a Unicorn. You've all been so nice to me, and it would be great to hang out with you guys every time I'm here visiting my new family. But there's this little problem."

"What problem could there possibly be? It all seems so simple. You want to be a Unicorn, and we want you to be one."

"The problem is Amy. See, she told your sister

last week that she wanted to be a Unicorn. Now she's claiming she really doesn't, but I think she's just covering up."

"Amy—a Unicorn?" Jessica was flabbergasted. "You must be joking."

"Isn't there any way you could consider making her an honorary member? I wouldn't feel right becoming one if she can't be one."

"Look, Amy is about as much of a Unicorn as my sister, and that's not even one percent. Let's face it—our sisters just aren't Unicorn material, and they never will be."

"But couldn't you just make an exception? Couldn't she just be a member while I'm one? After I'm gone, she could drop out of the club."

"Sorry, Ashley, but the Unicorns wouldn't go for it in a million years," Jessica said, wiping the sweat off her forehead. "Besides, we only want one new Unicorn. Not two."

"Well, then, how about if you make Amy one and not me?" Ashley suggested.

"Believe me, that won't be happening in this lifetime," Jessica said. *Maybe Ashley's just a little too nice for her own good*, she thought. *She really just doesn't understand that Amy is nowhere near cool enough to be a Unicorn.*

"Hey, guys! How was your rehearsal today?" Lila asked as Ashley and Jessica came out of the Sweet Valley Dance Studio.

"It was pretty grueling today," Jessica said. "But it was a good workout."

"I got my workout at the mall," Lila said.

"I guess your hand must get pretty tired from taking your Dad's credit card in and out of your wallet," Jessica commented.

"Very funny," Lila said.

"Did you find some good stuff today?" Ashley asked.

"Yeah, actually," Lila said brightly. "I got an adorable new dress and two pairs of jeans."

"Sounds great," Ashley said. "Nothing puts me in a better mood than buying great clothes."

"Why don't you come over to my house tonight, and I'll show you what I bought? All the Unicorns will be there. We're going to rent videos and order in pizza," Lila said.

"Oh, you have to come!" Jessica said excitedly. "It will be a lot of fun."

"I'd love to," Ashley said. "But I have a favor to ask you, Lila."

"Sure, what's up?"

"Is there any way you could invite Amy to come tonight? I know she'd really like it."

Jessica and Lila looked at each other as if Ashley had just suggested something totally unheard of. *She still doesn't get it that Amy just doesn't hang out with us,* Jessica thought.

"Hmmmm." Lila made an expression as if she were trying to figure out a hard math problem. "I guess it would be OK to have her come."

"Oh, that's great!" Ashley said excitedly.

"If Ashley's boring sister is coming, then my boring sister might as well come, too," Jessica said. "They can keep each other company."

"OK, you can both bring your sisters," Lila said. "Just don't let the word get around that I had non-Unicorns over to my house on a Saturday night. We do have a reputation to live up to."

"It's going to be a great night," Jessica said. "And the best part is that I'm going to bring my book of hairstyles so I can experiment on everyone's hair."

"That's a great idea," Ashley said. "I'm always looking for new things to do to my hair."

"I don't know, Jessica," Lila said, making a face. "I have to tell you that your hair's been looking just a little weird lately."

"I think Jessica's hair looks great," Ashley said.

"Thanks, Ashley," Jessica said, smirking at Lila. *I knew I liked this girl,* she thought.

"I have one more favor to ask you," Ashley said to Lila.

"Don't tell me—you want to bring your cousins and your aunt and uncle," Lila joked.

"Not quite," Ashley said, giggling. "I thought it might be nice if you called my dad's house this afternoon and invited Amy yourself. I know it would mean a lot to her."

"OK, it's a deal," Lila said.

"You must have caught Lila on a good day," Jessica teased. "She's never this nice."

"You're just getting funnier by the minute," Lila said. "And by the way, I'm a lot nicer than you think."

"Yeah, right," Jessica said. "I guess I just haven't gotten to know you very well in all these years we've been best friends!"

"Ashley! You won't believe it!" Amy shrieked on Saturday afternoon as she ran into her room. Ashley was sitting on one of the twin beds.

"What is it?" Ashley asked, looking up from a magazine.

"Lila just called, and she invited both of us to go over to her house tonight to watch videos and eat pizza with all the Unicorns."

"That sounds like fun," Ashley said. "I hope you told her we'd come."

"Of course I did," Amy said excitedly.

Ashley smiled. "You know, I kind of got the idea you didn't like the Unicorns."

"Oh, I just said that for Elizabeth's benefit the other day," Amy said dismissively. "She's really negative about them."

"I'm glad that's all it was. I really like those girls a lot," Ashley said.

Amy considered all the times in the past few days when she'd been angry at the Unicorns. *I was probably just overreacting when I said those things about them*, Amy thought happily. *They were probably just teasing me at Booster practice to show their acceptance. After all, they always tease one another.*

"I might be wrong about this," Amy said, "but I have a feeling that maybe they're inviting me because they want me to be a Unicorn. They've been looking for a new member. Why else would they invite me to hang out with them on a Saturday night?"

"Um, sure," Ashley said slowly. "You could be right."

Amy looked at her. *Why's she acting so wishy-washy? She could be a little more excited for me.*

"If they do ask me to become a member, I'll have to think of some way to explain it to Elizabeth," Amy continued. "I think it would really upset her if I became a Unicorn. She'd probably be afraid that I wouldn't be her friend anymore."

"Well," Ashley said, looking down at her hands, "maybe you won't even have to deal with that."

Ashley's weird mood was spoiling Amy's excitement. *Why is she acting so bummed over the idea that the Unicorns will ask me to be a member? Does she have to beat me at everything?*

Ten

◇

"Why in the world would I want to go to Lila Fowler's house and spend the evening with the Unicorns?" Elizabeth was sitting on her bed on Saturday afternoon while Jessica tried to convince her to go to Lila's. "I can think of about twenty things I'd rather do."

"Like what? Rearrange the books on your bookshelf? Study for a math quiz you have next year? Come on, Elizabeth, it's Saturday night. It'll be fun. And besides, Amy's going to be there."

"She is? How come?"

"Because Ashley didn't want to go unless Amy was invited, too," Jessica said. "You should have seen Lila's face when Ashley asked her if she could bring Amy. It was like Ashley had suggested that she give back all her dad's credit cards or something."

"I can't believe Lila agreed to let her come," Elizabeth said. "I know Lila's your best friend, but you have to admit that she's a total snob."

"You're right. She's a snob. But she said Amy could come to her house, so you have to come, too," Jessica said.

"Oh, I get it. Ashley's bringing her boring sister, so you thought you'd bring your boring sister, and the two of us boring sisters could keep each other company," Elizabeth said.

"Well, not exactly, but sort of."

Elizabeth laughed. "You are too much, Jessica Wakefield. But at least you're honest. OK, I'll come, but only because I want to do some scientific research."

"What kind of research?"

"I'm going to observe how silly and superficial young American girls can be when they're all together on a Saturday night," Elizabeth replied.

Jessica tossed her hair. "Well, Amy doesn't think we're silly. In fact, Ashley told me that she wants to be a Unicorn."

"How did that come up?"

"We asked Ashley to be a Unicorn, and she said that she didn't want to because she knew that Amy really wanted to be one. I explained to her that Amy would never be a Unicorn, but I don't think she gets it. I mean, the idea of Amy's becoming a Unicorn is totally ridiculous. How much more non-Unicorn can you get?"

"Me," Elizabeth suggested.

"Exactly."

Poor Amy, Elizabeth thought. *She wants to be a Unicorn, but they want her sister instead. I guess it's a good thing I'm going to Lila's—she'll need some support tonight.*

"I love your house, Lila," Amy gushed. "This is the biggest room I've ever been in."

"Thanks," Lila muttered nonchalantly.

It was Saturday night, and the Unicorns were sprawling in the Fowler family room along with Elizabeth, Amy, and Ashley. There were enough comfortable, oversized chairs and sofas to accommodate everyone. There were empty pizza boxes strewn around the room, and they had just finished watching a video. Amy was thrilled to be at Lila's and to show off such a beautiful mansion to her sister. She was starting to feel invisible again, though. It seemed as though the harder she tried to participate in the conversations, the more people ignored her.

"Ashley, why don't you and I give a little preview of *Sleeping Beauty*," Jessica suggested.

"I don't want to bore everyone," Ashley said.

"That's ridiculous," Janet told her. "We've all been hearing so much about what a great dancer you are, Ashley. I think it would be really cool to have our own private performance."

"Don't you guys want to watch another video?" Amy suggested.

All the girls except for Elizabeth and Ashley looked at Amy as if she'd just suggested they jump off the roof.

"That's a better idea," Ashley said, smiling at Amy. "I'm sure that'd be much more fun than watching us dance."

"It's not that I don't want to see you dance," Amy put in, not wanting to seem unappreciative. "I just don't want the surprise to be ruined. I want to wait and see the whole thing at the recital next week."

"I'm with you," Elizabeth agreed.

"This calls for a vote," Janet announced. "All those in favor of watching another video raise their right hand."

Amy looked around the room and saw that only she and Elizabeth had their hands raised. *Great. Now they probably think I don't care about my own sister.*

Ashley and Jessica stood up and started doing some steps from the ballet. *She really is talented,* Amy thought. Ashley was so graceful that she reminded Amy of a deer. *If I tried that, I'd look like a cow.*

When they'd finished their dance, everyone burst into applause. Amy forced herself to clap, too.

"That was awesome!" Mandy exclaimed.

"Ashley, you're like a professional dancer!" Tamara said. "I've never seen anyone your age who's so good."

"You make it seem so easy," Grace said. "I wish I could be that light on my feet."

"Thanks," Ashley said, obviously embarrassed by all the praise.

Seeing how impressed everyone was by her sister's performance, Amy had an image of her father at Ashley's recital. She imagined his face glowing with pride and love as Ashley took her bow. The image made Amy feel sick to her stomach. How could she possibly endure that moment? *Maybe I'm an evil person*, Amy worried. *I almost wish something would happen to keep Ashley from dancing in that recital.*

"Hold still," Jessica commanded Mary Wallace. The girls had moved upstairs to Lila's enormous bedroom, and Jessica was trying out different hairstyles on everyone. "If you keep moving your head around, this will never work."

"You keep digging into my scalp with that barrette," Mary complained. "Can't you be a little more gentle?"

Elizabeth was bored. Watching her sister doing the Unicorns' hair wasn't her idea of a good time. "What is that hairstyle supposed to be?" she asked.

"It's called a Romanian Roll," Jessica said. "It's very avant-garde."

"I've seen women in New York with hair like that," Ashley said.

"See? They're wearing this look in New York," Jessica said proudly. "I'm right on the cutting edge."

"Romanian Roll sounds like something they'd serve in the school cafeteria," Amy joked.

Ashley laughed, and Elizabeth forced a giggle. The Unicorns just stared. *Amy's been trying all night to be funny*, Elizabeth thought. *And no wonder— they're treating Ashley like a minor celebrity.* Amy's just trying to keep up.

"Ashley, let me show you my closets," Lila said, leading Ashley toward two huge rooms that were stuffed with more clothes than you could find at a department store.

Amy sat down on Lila's bed next to Elizabeth. "It's sick how Lila's showing off for Ashley," she whispered. "She's treating Ashley like she's a visiting princess or something."

"That's just Lila," Elizabeth whispered back. "Don't let her get to you."

"Why does one person need all those clothes, anyway?" Amy asked. "She's so spoiled."

If you disapprove of her, why are you trying so hard to be her friend? Elizabeth wanted to ask.

"OK, who wants to be my next victim?" Jessica asked. "Elizabeth? What about you? You could use a makeover."

"Thanks for the compliment, Jess, but I'm happy with my hair just the way it is," Elizabeth said. "Besides, I wouldn't let you get near me with that brush."

"I think that's a wise decision," Mary said, holding her head. "I have a splitting headache now."

"Well, your hair looks fabulous, Mary," Jessica said. "And that's all that matters."

"You can do my hair," Amy volunteered.

"Step right up," Jessica said, pointing to the chair in front of Lila's vanity. "When I'm done, you won't be able to recognize yourself in the mirror."

"Are you sure you want her to do this?" Elizabeth asked Amy before she got up from the bed.

"Of course I'm sure."

Elizabeth sighed. No matter how silly or snobby Amy thought the Unicorns were, she obviously really wanted to fit in.

"I'm going to give you something called a Moroccan Moment," Jessica said, studying her book of hairstyles.

Elizabeth rolled her eyes and began flipping through a magazine. She wasn't really interested in her sister's work in progress.

Ashley came back into the bedroom after her tour of Lila's closets. "Lila has the best clothes. You'd be a big hit in New York."

"I'd love to come visit you in New York sometime," Lila said.

"Maybe we should organize a Unicorn trip to visit Ashley," Janet said.

"That's a great idea!" Tamara said.

"I would absolutely love that," Ashley said. "And, Amy, you'd have to come, too, of course."

"I wouldn't miss it," Amy said.

"Ta-da!" Jessica said when she'd finished Amy's hair. "Behold the lovely Amy Sutton."

Elizabeth looked up from her magazine to see her friend's hairstyle. There was a pile of curls on top of Amy's head that was about a foot high.

Everyone burst into hysterical laughter except for Elizabeth and Ashley. Amy looked as though she was about to cry.

"You look like a poodle," Lila said between gasps.

"I'll pay you twenty dollars if you go out on the streets like that," Tamara teased.

"I think she looks really pretty," Ashley said, walking toward Amy and putting her hand on her shoulder.

"Excuse me," Amy said timidly. Then she jumped up from the chair and ran out of the room.

"We were only teasing," Janet yelled to Amy on her way out of the room.

Eleven

"OK, Elizabeth, I'm going to read the first part of my essay to you, and I want you to tell me what you think," Jessica said on Sunday afternoon. The girls were sitting at a table by the pool doing their homework. Steven was lying in a lounge chair a few yards away, soaking up the sun.

"I'd love to hear it," Elizabeth said, looking up from her math homework.

"I personally think it's really incredible. I've had a great time writing it," Jessica said.

"Wow, that's a first," Steven said without opening his eyes. "Jessica Wakefield had fun doing homework. Maybe we should call the local television station and have them do a story about it."

"I'm sorry," Jessica said to Steven, "but I don't believe your name is Elizabeth. And please keep your opinion to yourself. Nobody was talking to you in the first place."

"Come on," Steven said. "I'm dying to hear your essay. I didn't know you could actually read *and* write."

"Ha ha ha," Jessica said sarcastically.

"Just ignore him and read your essay," Elizabeth instructed.

"It turns out I'm a better writer than I thought," Jessica said. "But I want you to be honest. After all, you're the writer in the family."

"I'll be honest," Elizabeth said.

Jessica cleared her throat. "The title of my essay is 'Johnny Buck Is My Hero.'"

Steven started laughing so hard that the whole lounge chair started shaking. "Are you kidding? Is this a joke, or are you really writing an essay for school about Johnny Buck?"

Jessica was furious. Steven was always teasing her about Johnny Buck—he considered Johnny a bad singer and actor, and he loved to tell Jessica he thought so. "This is not a joke," she snapped at him, "and if you don't shut up, I'm going to go get Dad."

"Ignore him, Jess," Elizabeth repeated.

"I can't read it to you if he's here," Jessica said. "Let's go inside the house."

"I'm not going in the house," Elizabeth protested. "I'm all set up here with my homework, and it's a beautiful day. Just pretend like Steven's not here."

"OK, but one more word out of you, Steven

Wakefield, and I'm getting Dad," Jessica warned.

"Fine," Steven said. "My lips are sealed. Read your essay. I'm fascinated to know why Johnny Yuck, I mean Johnny Buck, is your hero."

Jessica cleared her throat again and started to read. "Johnny Buck is the person I admire the most. I have been a fan of his for as long as I can remember. Not only is he a fabulous singer, but he's also the best actor in the world—"

Jessica stopped reading and turned to glare at Steven, who was covering his mouth to stifle his laughter. His body was shaking.

"I warned you, Steven," Jessica said angrily.

"I'm sorry, but do you honestly think he's the best actor in the world?" Steven asked.

"That's what I wrote, and that's what I think. Now, keep your mouth shut, or I'm going to stuff my notebook in it."

"Come on, Steven, just let Jessica read her essay in peace so I can finish my homework," Elizabeth said.

"OK, OK. I'll be quiet," Steven said.

Jessica read again from her notebook. "I have every CD that Johnny Buck has ever recorded. When I hear his songs I feel like he's singing to me. He has a beautiful voice and I think he's the most handsome man I've ever seen. . . ."

Steven fell out of his lounge chair from laughing so hard. "You've got to be kidding," he said, gasping for breath.

Elizabeth tried not to smile. "Actually, Jess, he does have a point about the handsome part."

"What? I can't believe you're siding with Steven," Jessica said in outrage.

"It's just that I don't think Mrs. Arnette is going to appreciate knowing how handsome you think Johnny Buck is," Elizabeth explained. "It's not exactly her thing."

"What about the rest of the essay?" Jessica asked.

"I think it's pretty good," Elizabeth said. "But maybe you should find out a little more about his career. You know, make it kind of a research paper, so it's a little more academic."

"Yeah, and a little less moronic," Steven said from his position on the ground.

"Elizabeth, come here and help me do something," Jessica said.

Elizabeth smiled. She followed Jessica to the side of the pool, and on the count of three, they lifted Steven and heaved him into the water.

"So what do you want to write your article about?" Amy asked Ashley on Sunday afternoon. They were sitting in the Suttons' family room, and Amy was going to teach Ashley how to write a newspaper article.

"I want to write an article about how clean Sweet Valley is compared with New York," Ashley said. "Do you think that's a good idea?"

"It's a great idea," Amy said. "Is it really that much cleaner here?"

"About a million times cleaner," Ashley replied. "New York is the worst in the summertime, when all the garbage starts smelling up the streets."

"Yuck, how disgusting," Amy said, making a face. "How can you stand it?"

"I guess you just get used to it after a while," Ashley said. "I try not to breathe through my nose when I'm walking in the summer."

"Do people litter on the streets?"

"Are you kidding? I can't walk down one block without seeing trash and soda cans all over the ground," Ashley said. "People are so lazy. You'd think it wouldn't be that hard to throw your trash in the garbage can, but so many people don't."

"I guess people are more conscientious here," Amy said.

"That's what I want to talk about in my article. So how do I start?"

"You want to draw the reader in right from the beginning," Amy advised. "And you want to establish what it's about in the first paragraph."

"That sounds pretty simple. I'll start writing. Then I'll read you the first paragraph, and you can tell me what you think. And I want you to be honest."

"It's a deal," Amy said.

Amy watched as Ashley furrowed her brow in concentration. She loved being Ashley's teacher.

Ashley was so respectful, and Amy enjoyed having her admiration.

"OK, can I read what I have so far?" Ashley asked after a few minutes had passed.

"That was fast," Amy said, looking up from her math book. "Go ahead."

Ashley cleared her throat and read from her notebook. "This is an article about how dirty New York City is compared with Sweet Valley. I'm going to talk about how gross the streets in New York are and how clean they are in Sweet Valley. I think it's really a shame that people in New York don't take better care of the city that they live in."

Ashley put down her notebook and looked at Amy. "What do you think?"

I think it's terrible, but I can't say that, Amy thought. She couldn't help feeling slightly pleased that Ashley wasn't a good journalist. "It's a good first start, but I think instead of saying what you're going to write about, just start writing about it."

"What do you mean?" Ashley asked, a confused expression on her face.

"Just jump right into it from the beginning. Start describing a walk down a street in Sweet Valley and what you see. Then describe a walk down a New York City street."

"That's a great idea," Ashley said. "You're the best teacher!"

Amy had never thought of herself as a good teacher before, but she liked the idea a lot. She went back to her math book while Ashley made another attempt at her article.

"OK, here's my second try," Ashley said after a little while.

"Let's hear it," Amy said.

Ashley read from her notebook, "Sweet-smelling flowers, beautifully manicured green lawns, and children playing in the yard—these are what you find on a street in Sweet Valley. Wadded-up newspaper, empty fast-food containers, and soda cans in the gutter—that's what you see on a street in New York."

"That's a great first paragraph!" Amy exclaimed. "You're really catching on."

"You really think so?" Ashley asked excitedly. "Are you being honest?"

"I promise. I think that's really terrific."

"Alright!" Ashley exclaimed, her face glowing. "You have no idea how much it means to me to have your approval."

And you have no idea how much it means to me to be able to help you learn how to do something, Amy thought happily.

"How do you eat this?" Ashley asked, pointing to the artichoke on the plate in front of her.

"Here, watch me," Amy instructed. "You pull off a leaf like this, dip it in this yummy butter sauce, then scrape it off with your teeth." Amy was thrilled to show Ashley how to do something else—

even something as silly as eating an artichoke.

It was Monday night, and the Suttons and Ashley were celebrating Ashley's visit at La Maison Jacques, the fanciest restaurant in Sweet Valley.

"Once you've tried your first artichoke, you'll be addicted for life," Mrs. Sutton said.

"So how are rehearsals going for your recital?" Mr. Sutton asked Ashley.

Amy felt the familiar pang in her stomach. Somehow her father's interest in Ashley's ballet talent always did that to her. *Oh, get over it*, she told herself. *It's totally normal for Dad to be excited about Ashley's recital.*

"They're going pretty well, I guess. I'm just nervous about learning all the steps before Wednesday night."

"I have no doubt in my mind that you'll be fabulous," Mr. Sutton said. "Your mother told me that you were practically a professional dancer."

"I'm so sorry I'm not going to be able to come to your recital," Mrs. Sutton said. "Unfortunately, I'm going to be working on a story Wednesday night. I just hate that I'm going to miss it."

"Amy and I will be there," Mr. Sutton said. "I wouldn't miss it for the world—my own daughter dancing the lead in *Sleeping Beauty*."

Amy felt her heart drop despite herself. *He's talking like she's his only daughter—at least the only one who's doing anything important.*

"I hope I don't disappoint you," Ashley said. "What if I fall flat on my face?"

"You could never disappoint me," Mr. Sutton said.

Amy swallowed hard and tried to smile. "I can't wait, either." She looked across the table at her father. He was beaming with pride. *So why am I dreading Wednesday night more than I've ever dreaded anything in my life?* she thought.

"How's your essay going?" Ashley asked Amy on their way to school on Tuesday morning.

"Really well," Amy lied. The truth was that she'd been having a hard time writing anything at all. "How about yours?"

"I'm almost finished," Ashley said. "I can't wait for you to read it."

"Me either," Amy said, although she was looking forward to reading Ashley's essay about as much as she was looking forward to Ashley's dance recital—not at all. Amy hated the thought that Ashley's essay had come so easily for her, while she was having such a tough time. She didn't want to see any more evidence of her sister's talents.

"Listen, I was thinking that I could help you with your science homework this afternoon," Ashley offered as they approached the school. "I had so much fun yesterday when you were helping me learn how to write an article. I want to return the favor."

"Actually, you don't need to. I'm not really having any trouble," Amy said defensively. "In fact, I think it's pretty easy." The opposite was true— Amy was totally confused by all the stuff about ions and protons, and she was secretly worried that she wouldn't do well on the test later that week.

"Oh, OK," Ashley said dejectedly. "Let me know if you change your mind and you want some help."

Amy had a flash of her father's face the night before at the restaurant. "I won't change my mind, and I don't need any help," she said curtly. She couldn't bear to stand there another minute and see Ashley's confused and hurt expression. *How can I be so mean to her when she's been sweet to me ever since she got here?* She ran quickly up the stairs and into the school.

"There's Jessica holding court," Elizabeth said to Amy as she pointed down the hallway, where Jessica was surrounded by a bevy of boys. It was Tuesday afternoon, and Elizabeth and Amy were standing at Elizabeth's locker.

"I can't believe that doesn't bother you," Amy said.

"Doesn't what bother me?"

"Seeing your sister with so many adoring boys around her all the time. I mean, I know you realize you and Jessica are different people and everything, but don't you get jealous that she's so popular with the guys?"

Elizabeth laughed. "No way. Jessica's the boy-crazy twin in the family. It makes her happy to have all the guys like her. I could seriously care less."

"But don't you sometimes wish you got all that attention?"

"I get attention for things that are important to me," Elizabeth explained. "I'm happy if somebody has something nice to say to me about an article I wrote or if I got a good grade on a paper."

"You wouldn't want to trade places with Jessica for even a day?"

"Not for even an hour," Elizabeth said. "And there's enough room in this school for both of us and our differences."

Twelve

"Bravo! Bravo!" The auditorium was full of thunderous applause as the dancers took their bows. Ashley was standing in the center of the stage, and members of the audience were throwing long-stemmed red roses at her feet.

"She's so beautiful," someone sitting behind Amy said.

"She's the best Sleeping Beauty that's ever danced," another person sitting nearby said.

Amy ran up on the stage to give Ashley a big hug, but when she got there, Ashley was hugging their father. "You were wonderful," Amy called to her. "I'm so proud of you."

Neither her father nor Ashley looked at Amy. "You've made me so happy, Ashley," Mr. Sutton said, as tears streamed down his face. "You're the best daughter in the whole world."

"What about me?" Amy asked. "Aren't I the best daughter in the world, too?"

Mr. Sutton didn't respond. He took Ashley by the hand and led her off the stage. Amy stood there alone. "What about me?" she asked over and over again as she watched them walk away together.

Amy woke up suddenly and felt a damp spot on her pillow where she'd been crying. *It was only a dream. I'm not invisible, and Dad does love me.*

When she remembered it was Wednesday morning, she wanted to go right back to sleep. She pulled the covers over her head and thought about the day ahead of her. For one thing, her essay was due tomorrow, and she'd barely written a word—and for another, tonight was Ashley's recital.

She sat up and looked over at the bed where Ashley was still sleeping. *She looks so sweet and innocent,* Amy thought. For a moment Amy recognized her own features in her sister's face. *I do love her, and I am glad she's my sister.* But even though she adored Ashley, she still felt that gnawing jealousy. Amy had never felt so torn about anything before.

Amy walked into the bathroom to get a glass of water. When she looked in the mirror, she was filled with horror—right in the middle of her forehead was an enormous pimple. *How will I ever get through this day?* Amy wondered.

"That's a fantastic article about you, Ashley," Janet gushed. "You're a total celebrity today."

"You look beautiful in that photo they used," Ellen said. "You're so photogenic."

"Thanks," Ashley said, blushing. It was Wednesday, and everyone was swarming around the table in the cafeteria where Amy, Elizabeth, and Ashley were eating their lunch. The new copy of the *Sixers* had come out that morning, and the article about Ashley was a big hit.

Elizabeth noticed that Amy was looking more and more annoyed. *I should never have written that stupid article*, Elizabeth thought. *I knew Amy was feeling jealous of Ashley. This is probably just making her feel worse.*

Elizabeth had tried to cancel the article altogether, but Amy had insisted she go ahead with it. She assured Elizabeth that she was over her jealousy. But judging by the look on Amy's face, she was far from over it.

"Do you think you could sign my copy of the *Sixers*?" Winston Egbert asked Ashley.

"Sure," Ashley said, taking Winston's paper. "Don't you want Elizabeth to sign it, too? After all, she wrote the article."

"No, that's OK. I only want your autograph," Winston said.

"Gee, thanks a lot," Elizabeth said, pretending her feelings were hurt.

"It's not like Ashley's a movie star," Amy snapped.

Everyone looked at Amy. She looked surprised

herself. "Sorry, I'm in a funny mood today."

"Don't worry about it," Ashley told her. "You're right—I'm not a movie star."

"Hey," Ken Matthews said as he sat down at their table. "Great article, Ashley."

"Elizabeth wrote it," Amy pointed out, obviously irritated that her sort-of boyfriend was paying attention to Ashley.

"It was well written, Elizabeth," Ken said. "And you were lucky you had such a great subject to write about."

Amy pushed herself a little away from the table—and spilled her milk all over Ken's lap.

"I'm so sorry!" she shrieked. "I'm so clumsy."

"That's OK, it was an accident," Ken said, grabbing a handful of napkins.

There's no way that was an accident, Elizabeth couldn't help thinking as she watched Ken walk away.

Amy walked home from school on Wednesday afternoon with an overwhelming sense of doom. *What if my nightmare comes true? What if Dad realizes tonight that he only has room in his heart for one daughter?*

Amy couldn't remember the last time she had felt so sad. She knew she should be excited for her sister—tonight was her big night. And Ashley would be excited for her if *she* had some kind of big event. She was so proud of Amy's writing, after all.

As she walked into her house, she slammed the door so hard that a framed picture of her fell on the hallway floor. The sight of the broken picture—taken of Amy on a swing set when she was only four—made her feel even sadder. Part of her longed for the time when she was still an only child like the little girl in the cracked frame.

She trudged into the kitchen and threw her backpack on the floor. As she headed toward the refrigerator to find a snack, she noticed a note in the middle of the kitchen table.

Amy unfolded the note and read it. "Dear Amy and Dad—" Amy felt a chill go up her spine when she read that word. "The recital is now going to be held at the Sweet Valley High auditorium at seven thirty. There was a scheduling problem at the middle-school auditorium, so there was a last-minute change. I can't wait to see you both there. All my love, Ashley."

"Hello? No, this is Amy. The recital is at seven thirty in the Sweet Valley High auditorium." Amy was sitting in the kitchen trying desperately to finish her essay, but the phone kept ringing and interrupting her. About a dozen people had called for Ashley to find out about the recital that night, and Amy was about to lose her patience.

Amy sat back down at the kitchen table after the last annoying call and picked up her pen. Three seconds later, the phone rang again. She threw her pen down on the table and stomped across the room to pick up the phone.

"Ashley's residence!" she said tersely into the receiver.

"Hi, Amy, it's Ashley. That's a funny way to answer the phone."

"Oh, hi," Amy said, startled by Ashley's voice on the other end. "I was just joking around."

"I wanted to make sure you saw the note I left for you and Dad on the kitchen table."

Dad! There's that word again, Amy thought as she felt that gnawing feeling in her stomach. "Yeah, I saw it."

"Oh, good. And will you make sure that Dad sees it?"

"Of course," Amy said.

"Well, I better go back to rehearsal. I can't wait to see you tonight!"

"Me, too," Amy said. "And Ashley, good luck tonight."

"Thanks. I'll need it."

Amy hung up the phone and sat back down at the table. The note loomed before her, and she couldn't concentrate on her essay. The dream she'd had that morning kept playing itself over in her head. When the phone rang again, she didn't answer it. Instead, she grabbed the note, crumpled it into a ball, and threw it in the garbage can.

"Before you say you're tired of hearing about

my hair, I have to ask you one really important question," Jessica said to Elizabeth on Wednesday evening. Jessica was getting ready for the dance recital in her bedroom. Elizabeth was sitting on Jessica's bed.

"If you ask me about your hair one more time I'm not going to talk to you for a week. I'm not kidding. I've been hearing about your hair so much lately that I'm starting to have nightmares about it," Elizabeth said.

"I told you not to say that," Jessica said.

"I said it anyway."

"You have to make an exception tonight," Jessica said. "I have to look perfect in the recital."

"Really? I didn't know that was part of it. I thought you just had to *dance* perfectly."

"Come on, just tell me if you think I should wear my hair in a plain bun or in a braided bun."

Elizabeth sprawled out on the bed, exhausted. Obviously, there was no way she'd be able to get out of giving her opinion. "I think you should wear it in a braided bun. Just for variety."

"That's a good point," Jessica said. "I will."

"I'm really looking forward to your recital," Elizabeth said. "I bet you'll be great."

"Wait until you see Ashley dance. What you saw her do at Lila's is nothing compared with what she'll do tonight. She's really awesome. I still can't believe she and Amy are sisters," Jessica said as she started to braid her hair.

"What do you mean?"

"Ashley's so much cooler than Amy," Jessica said. "She's so pretty and popular and sophisticated."

"I think Amy is all those things," Elizabeth said. She hated it when Jessica put her friend down—especially since Amy had so many inferior feelings herself.

"And Amy's been acting pretty weird lately," Jessica continued, trying to see the back of her head in the mirror. "She was so goofy, making all those dumb jokes at Lila's house."

"You know, Jess, your friends can be pretty intimidating," Elizabeth said. "I think she was just nervous, and she wanted everyone to like her."

"Well, she shouldn't try so hard," Jessica said. "People are always trying so hard to impress us Unicorns. It's such a turn-off."

"Jessica, you sound as if you think the Unicorns are some kind of royalty," Elizabeth said.

Jessica tilted her head thoughtfully. "Well, we kind of are."

Elizabeth burst out laughing. "You're really too much."

"Thanks. So how does it look?" Jessica asked. "Does it look OK from the back?"

"It's beautiful," Elizabeth said. "Now don't ask me another question about it."

"OK." Jessica did a dramatic leap across the room. "Wish me luck."

"Good luck," Elizabeth said as Jessica flew out her bedroom door.

Elizabeth sat for a few moments on Jessica's bed. She wasn't sure why, but she had a bad feeling about Amy. *I hope Amy makes it through this night,* she thought.

Thirteen

Amy sat up straight in her bed and looked at the alarm clock on her night table. It was six thirty. She had fallen into a deep sleep and was supposed to be at Elizabeth's in forty minutes so that they could go to Ashley's recital together.

She jumped out of bed and was starting to change her clothes to get ready when she stopped in her tracks with a feeling of horror. *The note. I threw away the note.*

Amy heard her father walking around downstairs. *He didn't see the note because it's crumpled in the trash can,* she thought. *He's down there right now, and he has no idea that the place of the recital has been changed. Dad would never in a thousand years imagine that I would be capable of doing something as rotten as keeping him from Ashley's recital on purpose.*

Amy was rushing around looking for her favorite pink sweater, but she couldn't find it anywhere. *Maybe Ashley borrowed it without telling me*, Amy thought. She walked across the room to the bureau where Ashley was keeping her clothes. The pink sweater was nowhere to be found.

When Amy glanced over at Ashley's bed, she noticed Ashley's blue notebook—the same notebook she'd been writing her essay in. Before she realized what she was doing, Amy had opened the notebook in search of the essay about their father.

There! she thought, coming to the page. As she started to read, her heart almost stopped. It wasn't about her father at all—it was about Amy!

My sister, Amy Sutton, is the person I admire the most. Although I've only known her for a short time, I feel like I've known her my whole life.

Amy and I only recently discovered that we were half sisters, and that discovery is one of the best things that's ever happened to me. From the first moment I stepped off the plane, Amy welcomed me with open arms. She treated me like a sister right from the start. We found out that we had so much in common. In fact, I feel like I have more in common with her than with anyone in the world.

Amy has a great sense of humor, and she makes me laugh all the time. She's so natural and comfortable with herself that she makes everyone she comes in contact with feel comfortable, too. There's nothing fake or superficial about her.

She's so talented in many different ways. She's a great writer and will be a great journalist when she grows up if that's what she wants to be. She's a wonderful teacher and has an amazing amount of patience. She's also a serious student and a terrific athlete. Above all else, she's a loyal friend, daughter, and sister.

I feel truly lucky that I have found my sister, Amy, after all these years, and I look forward to knowing her and loving her for the rest of my life.

Amy's hands were shaking. She felt warm tears streaming down her face, and she hugged the notebook to her chest. *I'm a terrible person,* Amy thought. *Ashley loves me, and I love her, and I've been so stupid.*

She glanced down and saw her pink sweater underneath her own bed. The sight of the sweater made her feel even guiltier than ever.

She threw on the sweater and ran into the bathroom to splash cold water on her face. *I have to tell Dad about the recital!*

"Dad!" Amy yelled as she bounded down the stairs. "Dad! Where are you?"

Amy felt her heart pounding as she flung Mr. Sutton's study door open. He wasn't there. She ran into the kitchen. He wasn't there, either.

"Dad!" she yelled again. In a panic, Amy picked up the phone and called her father's office, but he wasn't there. She tried her mother's office, but nobody answered. She looked out in the driveway and saw that his car was gone. *It's too early for him to have left for the recital. He must be making a stop first. But where?*

Amy reached into the garbage in the kitchen and pulled out the note. She tried to smooth out the wrinkles so it wouldn't look as if it had been crumpled up. She put it back on the table in the same spot where she had found it. *Please, Dad, come home and find that note,* she pleaded.

I have to find Dad. I have to find Dad, Amy kept repeating to herself. She was frantically riding her bike around the streets of Sweet Valley. She looked at her watch every two minutes—the recital was going to start in half an hour and her father was nowhere in sight.

Pedaling as fast as she could, Amy looked in the parking lot at the Valley Mall, but she didn't see her father's car. She pedaled past the dry cleaner's, the bakery—every possible place she could think of.

The sound of thunder rumbled in the distance, and Amy felt a drop of rain on her head. Within minutes, she found herself in the middle of a downpour. Rain mingled with her tears as she rode furiously up and down the residential streets.

Amy imagined Ashley's disappointed face when she realized her father wasn't in the audience. *When Ashley finds out what I've done, she'll never want to talk to me again. She'll take back every nice thing she wrote about me in that essay. She'll realize that I'm a terrible, awful person and she won't want to be my sister.*

And how would she ever explain what she'd done to her father? He'd never understand how she could hurt him and Ashley like that. *He'll ground me for the rest of my life. He'll wish that he only had one daughter—Ashley.*

Amy biked to the Wakefields' house. She let her bike fall to the ground on their front lawn. She ran breathlessly up the steps and pounded on the door.

"Amy!" Elizabeth gasped when she opened the door. "What's wrong with you? You're soaking wet. Have you been crying?"

"I've done something terrible," Amy cried. "I need your help, but we don't have much time."

"Come inside and tell me what's going on."

They stood in the hallway while Amy explained the whole situation. By the time she'd finished, there was a puddle on the floor from all the rain that had dripped from her hair and clothes.

"Listen, Amy, I'll get on my bike, and between the two of us, I'm sure we'll find your dad," Elizabeth reassured her. "Don't worry. I know this is going to work out."

"Thanks, Elizabeth, you're the best friend anyone

could ever have," Amy said, wiping away a tear. "I'll see you at the auditorium."

"We better hurry," Elizabeth said, looking at her watch. "Time is running out."

Amy stood at the back of the auditorium in Sweet Valley High and searched up and down the rows for her father. He wasn't there. *Of course he isn't here*, she thought miserably. *He isn't here because of my stupid jealousy.*

She walked slowly toward an empty seat in the back just as the lights were going down. One by one the dancers appeared on the stage.

Amy swelled with pride when she saw Ashley appear. She looked more beautiful than ever in her pale-pink tutu. When she did her long solo, she looked like a bird flying across the stage. She turned and leaped with such grace that it took Amy's breath away.

She's so talented, she thought proudly. Suddenly Elizabeth's advice to her, and what Ashley wrote in her essay, really hit home. *It's OK that Ashley's a good dancer and I'm not. Ashley admires me because I'm me— there's no point trying to be anyone else. And I can love her even though she's better at some things than I am.*

As the dance ended, the auditorium filled with applause. Ashley was beaming as she took her elegant bow. Amy leaped to her feet and clapped harder than she'd ever clapped in her life. She was so happy for Ashley, and this time she loved hearing all the applause.

But a terrible feeling quickly washed away her joy. *If only Dad could have been here*, she thought sadly. *He would have been so happy to see Ashley dance tonight. This would be a perfect moment if I hadn't messed everything up.*

Fourteen

"Bravo! Bravo!" A loud voice was shouting above all the rest from the front of the room.

Amy walked toward the stage to find Ashley and congratulate her after the performance. *How will I explain to her why Dad isn't here?* Amy worried as she scanned the front of the room for her sister.

The booming voice shouting "Bravo" was getting louder as Amy made her way to the front of the room. She spotted Ashley smiling at someone in the audience. She watched as her sister ran to one of the rows and threw her arms around someone. *Dad! He's here.*

Amy's father had made it to the recital after all. Amy saw the two of them hugging each other. Then they pulled apart and searched the room for something. Suddenly Amy realized what they were looking for—they were looking for her.

Amy ran toward her sister and father, and the two of them swept Amy up in their embrace. "I'm so proud of you, and I love you so much," Amy said to Ashley. "You were so wonderful up there tonight."

"Thank you," Ashley said breathlessly.

"I'm so proud of both of my daughters," Mr. Sutton said.

"Ashley was great tonight, don't you think?" Amy asked Elizabeth. "She's such an incredible dancer."

The Wakefields were having a party at their house after the ballet on Wednesday night. All the dancers and their families were gathered in the living room for cider and cookies. Ashley and Jessica, who had the second-biggest role, were definitely the stars of the night. Elizabeth was worried that Amy would be jealous of all the attention Ashley was getting at the party.

"She was terrific," Elizabeth said. "I hope you're not upset about how much attention she's getting."

"Upset?" Amy asked, smiling. "I'm totally thrilled."

"That's a turnaround," Elizabeth said, surprised but pleased.

"Yeah, well, I finally realized that everything you were saying to me was true. It's OK for Ashley to be good at ballet. Let's face it, ballet just isn't my thing. And neither are the Unicorns. I have to admit that Ashley's more Unicorn-like than I am."

Elizabeth let out a sigh of relief. "Wow, I was beginning to get worried there."

"Well, you've definitely helped me come to my senses," Amy said, reaching for a cookie. "And you also get full credit for getting my father to the recital on time. I don't know what I would have done without you tonight. It would have been a disaster if he hadn't made it."

"I guess I did make a pretty good guess about finding him at the middle-school auditorium. Luckily, he was pulling his car into the parking lot just as I drove my bike by the school."

Amy squirmed nervously. "Did you tell him about how I threw the note away?"

Elizabeth shook her head. "I didn't think that was any of my business. I just told him that the place was changed, and he didn't ask any more questions."

"Thanks a million," Amy said. "I owe you one."

"Are you going to tell him about the note?" Elizabeth asked, a concerned look in her eyes.

Amy looked at her cookie with a frown. "I haven't decided yet. I'm sure he'd be furious, and he would never understand how I could do something like that." She sighed and met Elizabeth's gaze. "But I also hate the idea of being dishonest with him. What do you think I should do?"

"I think you have to decide that one on your

own," Elizabeth said. "But I usually think it's best to be honest. Maybe it would be good to tell him about how bad you'd been feeling."

"You're probably right," Amy said, looking across the room at Mr. Sutton. "I'm just afraid of what his reaction might be."

Just then Madame André tapped on her glass of cider with a fork. "I'd like to propose a toast to Ashley. She saved the ballet tonight," Madame André said as she lifted a glass in the air. "If it weren't for her, I don't know what we would have done."

"Let's drink to our sisters!" Amy said to Elizabeth, raising her glass of cider.

"I'm really going to miss you, Ashley," Amy said on Thursday night after dinner. They were sitting on Amy's bed, and Ashley had just finished packing her bag for her departure the next day. "I wish you could stay longer. It's been so incredible having you here."

"I know. I feel the same way," Ashley said. "We've just gotten to know each other, and now I have to leave. But I want you to come and visit me in New York sometime soon."

"I'd love to," Amy said. "There's only one thing—I'd rather go when the Unicorns aren't going."

Ashley laughed. "No problem. I'd rather hang out just the two of us anyway. I'm so happy you're my sister, Amy. I just feel so lucky that you're in my life now. And I really feel like we've known each other forever."

"Me, too," Amy said. "Oh, my gosh! I almost forgot. I wanted to show you something."

Amy walked over to her bureau and pulled out two miniature porcelain ballet dancers. "Our grandmother gave these to me before she died. She said that her grandmother had given them to her when she was a little girl, and that's why she'd decided to become a ballerina."

"They're beautiful," Ashley said. She looked entranced as she took one of the dancers in her hand. "They're so little and delicate."

"I want you to have one," Amy said.

"Really? Are you sure?"

"I'm positive."

Ashley hugged Amy tightly, and for a minute Amy thought about telling her sister about throwing away the note. *Maybe I'll tell her when we have more time to talk about everything that went on*, she decided. *Right now it would only upset her.*

Amy stared out the window as she and her father were driving home from the airport. She was really sad to say good-bye to Ashley, but she knew she'd be seeing a lot more of her in the years to come. She looked over at her father. He looked sad, too. The two of them had barely said two words to each other since they'd gotten in the car.

Amy took a deep breath. "Dad, there's something I need to tell you."

"I think I know what you're going to say," Mr. Sutton said.

"You do?"

"Yes. I know about the note, and it's OK."

Amy was shocked. "But how do you know? Elizabeth told me she didn't say anything."

"She didn't. After her recital, Ashley told me she was glad I'd seen the note she'd left for us on the kitchen table."

"What did you say?" she asked in a small voice.

"I just acted like I'd seen it," Mr. Sutton said.

"I'm so sorry," Amy said. "I'm really a rotten daughter. I'll understand if you want to ground me."

"I'm not going to ground you," he said softly.

"You're not?"

"No, and in fact, I would understand if you wanted to ground me," Mr. Sutton said.

Amy stared at him. "What did *you* do wrong?"

"I haven't been all that sensitive to your feelings lately. When we first told you about Ashley, you were so happy, so I just assumed everything would be all right."

"But I really *was* happy to find out about Ashley," Amy protested. "I thought everything would be all right, too."

"Your mom and I were really relieved—we expected you to be more upset. So instead of paying closer attention to your feelings after Ashley arrived, you seemed so happy I just assumed you were handling it OK."

"But I guess I didn't really handle it OK." Amy spoke in a soft voice. "I got kind of jealous. And I sort of thought you wouldn't love me anymore if you had another daughter who was so beautiful and talented."

Mr. Sutton slowed the car at a stoplight and looked at her. "Oh, sweetheart, you're my little girl. I love you more than you could ever know. Nobody could ever change that."

Amy smiled. "You're the best dad in the world. I'm not jealous anymore. I'm glad Ashley's my sister, and I love her with all my heart."

"I know you do," Mr. Sutton said. "That makes me really happy."

"She wrote the most wonderful essay about me for social studies class," Amy went on, tears filling her eyes.

"And you wrote a wonderful essay about me."

Amy raised her eyebrows. "How do you know that?"

"Mrs. Arnette called this afternoon before we left for the airport and said that you'd written the best essay in the class. She wants to publish it in the *Sixers*."

"Are you serious?" Amy was so happy she was about to burst.

"Yes, I am." He reached another stoplight and covered her hand with his own. "I asked her to read it to me on the phone, and it moved me to tears. I am truly proud of you, Amy. I hope you know that."

Amy gave him a hug. "I do, and I'll never forget it as long as I live."

"It was really hard to say good-bye," Amy was telling Elizabeth on the phone later that evening.

"I'm so glad everything worked out OK," Elizabeth said.

Amy sighed. "So I guess now our lives will go back to normal," she said.

"Well, not totally normal," Elizabeth said. "Jessica has another juicy piece of gossip."

Amy laughed. "All right. Spill."

"Jess told me she overheard Mr. Bowman and Mr. Drew talking today," Elizabeth said. "It looks like the English department and the drama department are going to work together to put on a big production of *Romeo and Juliet*. Auditions start next week."

"Wow," Amy said. "That is big news."

"Jessica's already decided she's going to be Juliet," Elizabeth said with a giggle.

"What about you?" Amy asked.

"I figure I'm more of a behind-the-scenes type. I was thinking you and I could work on sets together," Elizabeth suggested.

"That sounds great," Amy said happily.

"Good," Elizabeth said. "Now let's just hope Jessica gets the part of Juliet, or she's going to turn our lives into a nightmare."

Will Jessica get to play Juliet in the middle-school play? Find out in Sweet Valley Twins 84, **ROMEO AND 2 JULIETS.**

We hope you enjoyed reading this book. If you would like to receive further information about available titles in the Bantam series, just write to the following address, with your name and address:

Kim Prior
Bantam Books
61–63 Uxbridge Road
Ealing
London W5 5SA.

If you live in Australia or New Zealand and would like more information about the series, please write to:

Sally Porter
Transworld Publishers
(Australia) Pty Ltd
15–25 Helles Avenue
Moorebank
NSW 2170
AUSTRALIA

Kiri Martin
Transworld Publishers (NZ) Ltd
3 William Pickering Drive
Albany
Auckland
NEW ZEALAND

SWEET VALLEY HIGH ™

The top-selling teenage series starring identical twins Jessica and Elizabeth Wakefield and all their friends at Sweet Valley High. One new title every month!

SWEET VALLEY HIGH™

THE SADDLE CLUB

Bonnie Bryant

Share the thrills and spills of three girls drawn together by their special love of horses in this adventurous series.